Provenance

a novel

Prejudice.
Love.
Naivete.
Deceit.

I dedicate this book to mindset—that imperfect feature that exists in all of us. We are not entirely without fault, as we are products from whence we come.

Yes, provenance.

Chapter One

*This dawn would unfurl an anthology buried by time.
The blood had dried—and with it, memories had been
repressed. Those living and dead would be resurrected,
their lives replayed in the self-described culpable
mind and disreputable soul of the Little Captain.*

DEPRESSING THE SNOOZE BUTTON would not ward off the
rigors of another day.

Following a night of tossing and turning, this day would,
by concession, start as so many others had. Introduced by
a contemptuous alarm, morning would resurrect a man
whose life was fortified by indentured conviction, unrecognized naivete, and travail. Although somewhat obscured
by time, the anguish of an indelible past would not only be
relived but redefined.

By rote, the old man begrudgingly turned his gnarled
torso and placed puffy, discolored, arthritic feet onto the

creaking floor. Introduced by a grimace, the anticipated pain raised groans that reverberated across the spartan room.

With a furrowed brow and a throat-clearing growl, he wrestled away sleep, shook his head, and looked across the room. Nothing had changed. He was alone—now always alone.

Although his room was not the Smithsonian, his pandering gaze was not unlike a perusal of America's Attic. Photos and artifacts hung on the walls. But these were not the annals of a nation. They were the relics of one man's experience, long since laid to rest.

The room was not without order. With each item appropriately positioned, it satisfied the criteria of being forlorn as well as arranged with near-impeccable feng shui. There was balance and a semblance of harmony. It was an enduring personification of its curator.

No matter in which direction one looked, a defining statement was made. The affirmation of a man bearing willful penance. The décor resonated somber tones. Alphabetically arranged hardbound classics leaned askew against a miniature of Rodin's *The Thinker*—consistent with the sculpted setting. Partially drawn pastel curtains and a path-worn area rug, both in fashion from another time and another place, served to expiate a life in need.

In a frame fashioned from the limb of *Hevea brasiliensis,* a watercolor of an ornate pink-and-white neoclassical building adorned the wall over his bed. Positioned on a bedside table were photographs of two young women— one blond and fair, the other copper skinned with ebony hair. As if concealing a secret, he placed a finger to his lips before touching each photo.

"Good morning," he whispered with a penitent smile.

Strengthened by a throaty life-goes-on "ho hum," he worked to stand erect with the help of his walking stick. Undulating linear shadows filled the room as the early morning sun entered through the latticed window. With a self-imposed flagellating frown, he equated this display with a bamboo cage to which he had been witness long ago, its bloodied floor blotted by time.

His current setting was made more cheerful by a frenzy of birds beneath the sill and the distinct *chirrup* of a resident cardinal. As a boy, he had prized birds. Their high-spirited sounds and vibrant colors were synonymous with peace and serenity. The juxtaposition of latticed shadows made it all the more meaningful.

Life's encounters are always legitimized and more poignant when offset by one's relative experience.

Shaking off the past, the man focused on the now-formidable task of getting dressed. He donned neatly pressed trousers and his favorite starched cotton jersey. An ascot neatly tucked into his collar covered a vexing, sagging neck on an aging, compromised habitus.

He looked in the mirror, adjusted his collar, and feigned approval before resuming a chiseled routine.

Standing outside on the front deck, he witnessed the morning with a look of satisfaction. Although fleetingly, he fancifully recalled a time when he could sally down the front steps.

Now, the task at hand: collecting the morning mail. Once approached with anticipation and zest, this endeavor was now carried out with a stippling of angst, lest there be something other than confounding bills and advertisements.

With his cane in one hand and the other arm extended as though walking along a rail, he made his way to the mailbox. He moved at a guarded, teetering pace. With tremulous hands, he gathered the mailbox's contents, tucking them beneath his arm while easing his way toward the Big-Sea-Water.

Before descending the red clay footpath to the rocky shore below, he stood motionless, scanning Gitche Gumee—an expanse he had chosen to call "the other inland sea." Closing his eyes, he took a deep breath. The morning air was crisp, refreshing. Just as it had been in days gone by.

Walking bent-kneed for balance, he wavered cautiously, stabilizing a foothold on a strategically placed yet precariously exposed root. Worn thin, it remained a key rung to the water's edge.

Brushing against a cedar tree, the man caught a fragrance reminiscent of his grandfather's sauna. When used as switches during the communal baths, cedar boughs would titillate the skin and soothe the soul.

Embraced as a traditional sanctuary, the sauna was a Saturday-night refuge for strict meditation, a place from which to gain strength and purity. It symbolized the biblical affirmation in which his grandparents took solace: that the afterlife would provide relief and reward for arduous days of labor. With this promise in mind, one could accept the day. Fortified and strengthened, one could face another rising sun.

But despite their perpetually renewed resolve, his grandparents still could not escape the reality that each day was abrasive. Neither could his own parents. And with that, the subliminal foundation had been laid. Unbeknownst to him, the Little Captain was in the mold, even at a time when his own days were simple, with smooth edges, without restriction.

Now perched awkwardly on a rock, the man leaned back to scan the water. With meandering thoughts, he could escape to a place nonthreatening and benign. He could find a sense of peace.

When he was young, Longfellow's "The Song of Hiawatha" made vivid this calm and placid water once flanked by wigwams and embraced by a canopy of dark pines. A littoral scene of tranquility. Fantasy brought comfort—childhood as it should be.

But now, estranged from society and penitent by choice, the man communicated with the world and its players only through soliloquy—neither judgmental nor threatening.

Intensifying his gaze, he looked out upon the offing, the steel-gray abyss that met the sky with nary a line. It was as if the antithesis of his life's narrative lay before him. There it was, the water with an unblemished and indiscernible transition into the sky. There was no beginning. There was no end. And there was nothing in between.

Certainly, life too should have its genteel horizons that allow day to steal unabated into night.

For Dr. Noah Garrett, however, life had been discordant, defined with irregular lines and broken borders, tortuous and conflicting. It was devoid of gentle folds, subliminal margins, and transitioning hues.

But this place offered restoration and peace.

Noah began his career as a neurosurgeon. Anticipated demands yet lucrative rewards. But then came a transition parlayed as payback and retribution. He became keeper of the town, a country doctor at the Laborville Community Hospital. Marginal rewards had been accepted. A dream laid to rest.

Sitting knock-kneed and feet apart for stability, Noah was undeterred by his tenuous perch on the rock. With liver-speckled hands, arthritic knuckles, and fingers conceded to ulnar deviation, he attempted to muster a grin as he found space to sort his mail. Sifting through the mix would give him something to do, even if no satiable fruit would come his way.

He arranged bills in a to-do pile, pitched hoodwinking classifieds in another pile, and placed modest social security and retirement checks into an all-too-small immediate-attention pile. Laborville's supplemental reward from the reservation had become a necessity. The compensation was a pittance for a job well done.

With concerned puzzlement, he raised one envelope toward the sky at arm's length as if to enhance the script. Squinting with a furrowed brow and questioning eyes, he could read, "Senhor Noah Garrett." The return address: Manaus, Brazil.

Senhor Noah—a moniker long forgotten.

It triggered a piercing chill.

He lowered his head and sucked air through clenched teeth while turning the envelope over and over in his tottering hands. Tightly closing his eyes with a blistering grimace, his spontaneous response was an audibly whispered "*Why?*"

He opened the onionskin envelope and removed a folded sheet of pastel-flowered paper. The script, exhibiting purposeful calligraphy, read:

> *Dear Senhor Garrett,*
>
> *This letter is written with resolve, yet it harbors an element of remorse. You must understand, I write because of the love and respect I share for two people.*
>
> *You must be informed that Sabella has died. I have been strengthened by her saga and never-ending quest to retain that which is our family's land and its riches. I know you served a special role in her mission to attain that end.*
>
> *Your presence in her life was more monumental than you have ever known. I know her story, and now I know yours. I must confess . . .*

Breathless, chest heaving, eyes wide, mouth agape, Noah was the portrait of distress and puzzlement.

"This can't be," he said to no one. "Not *my* story."

Struck by a torrent of piercing thoughts, he felt the ripping pangs of treachery once again entangled with loss. Confronting the same feelings he had first experienced so many years ago, he raised his head toward the sky, took a deep breath, and closed his eyes.

"Why? Oh my God . . . why?"

In that instant, he was in another place, another time. Before him lay the other inland sea.

Chapter Two

It remains axiomatic: progeny begets progeny.
Nascent molds, each shaped by convention or conflict,
may produce opposites—especially when they are
conceived worlds apart.

We are the product from whence we come.

THE LABORVILLE COMMUNITY HOSPITAL, catercorner from
Aston Park, was in the process of being transformed from
a company roadhouse into a makeshift medical facility. Its
configuration, austere and marginally functional, exhibited
a disjointed-matchbox appearance. Family physicians and
interns from the nearby Indian reservation, all bearing white
coats and deferments, scurried though the musty corridors.

The hospital served as a birthing center for those bound
to this northern Minnesota town. Its inanimate benefactors,
the open-pit Rickert Iron Mine and the Merritt Railroad,

served as Laborville's lifelines, much as their industries did for the entire country. Hematite ore was refined and reconfigured into fighting machines that would eventually lay waste and rust over foreign soil or sink beneath the vast oceans of the world.

The country was at war. For those called to duty, pressed army greens, navy whites, and air force blues proudly replaced the rusty-red coveralls still worn by those who remained shackled to the ferrum-rich earth.

But for Charles Garrett, a 4-F designation proved a castigating blemish, both demeaning and transforming. Indisposed with high blood pressure and a heart condition, he was an inglorious casualty, albeit far from the distant theaters of war.

His companions served nevertheless with enduring accolades, their banners held high. Charles could see them in his mind's eye but no longer touch them. Clem, his ruddy-complexioned brother-in-law, was a P-51 pilot who would wave his arms and smile as he pantomimed the wild blue yonder. Walt, a paratrooper—lovable, serious to a fault, and hands down the only choice for best man at his wedding—jumped at the Bulge. Eddie, his ninth-grade buddy and a dairy farmer from Twig, was on the aircraft carrier *Langley*.

None of them returned.

Day and night, the ground shook beneath Charles's feet, racking his soul, as men too old to be warriors detonated charges buried deep in the floor of the iron-rich Rickert mine. His medical status, compromised, didn't even allow him the dignity of working with other miners. Charles imagined that those remaining in Laborville looked at him and wondered, "Why are you here? Just keeping score?" All the shackles of imperfection and self-imposed shame were a burden he couldn't, or wouldn't, shed.

Charles veered from the ubiquitous prying eyes that sought nourishment in his festering guilt. Monday—wash day—was safe. On that day of the week, no judgmental eyes lurked the town, questioning why an apparently strapping man should remain out of harm's way. Women who gave their husbands to the war effort were not only busy grating their knuckles over washboards but also fabricating bomb-bay doors or driving rivets into the fuselages of B-29s.

Charles configured his sense of penance into a means by which to raise the Little Captain. Morning walks, hand in hand with his toddling son, served as a reprieve from his lancinating shame.

Kneeling, he tidied the Little Captain's sailor suit, adjusting the collar and repositioning the white cap, tilting it just a bit to mimic the fashion of the day. Marine attire heralding all three colors of Old Glory held special favor for this man left behind, this man who had not been granted an honorable truce from Laborville's pick-and-shovel existence.

"Perfect, just perfect." In lockstep, he poked a loving yet directional thumb into the Little Captain's back. "Walk straight and tall. You're my boy."

While fettered by a limited education and perceived as tarnished, Charles nevertheless wielded an innate personal resolve. He remained the fundamental architect of his own destiny. The Little Captain, as if positioned at orchestral level, watched and listened. The learning came naturally.

However imperfect, Charles was a man of integrity, driven with purpose. The same inflexibility would eventually bequeath adulation upon—and simultaneously tarnish—his only child.

Though nearly devoid of young men, Laborville was replete with their spouses, many of whom were caring for and shepherding small children. Under the cloak of war, most accepted the task with a sense of duty and even pride. However, others found it laborious and woefully oppressive—as was the case for the young Mrs. Garrett.

Severe and tumultuous and pummeled by poverty, her life had taken an even more distressing turn on a stormy April night four years previous. Not by her intended design, that was when she reluctantly entered Laborville Community Hospital, the sterile institution where she gave birth to what was initially more burden than blessing.

There was no way this swaddled child could realize his eventual career path would take a precipitous detour and reach its terminus at the renovated brick-and-mortar structure in which he had taken his first breath.

Since that inauspicious occasion four years earlier, Stella Garrett had perceived her life as one of indentured servitude. She became tethered to Charles's son, a child for whom she was unable to take ownership—not because of antipathy but because of simple incapability. A casualty of the Great Depression, she lived in a world comprised of and fraught with everything dire.

For her afternoon walks with Noah—the Little Captain, by Charles's chosen sobriquet—she would dress him per instruction or out of fear. She would restrain him with a tethering leash, lest he dart into the street and be run down, ending his life and hers.

"Keep a close eye on him," Charles would instruct. "You know he's rambunctious. Don't let him run into the street. Don't forget—he's your responsibility."

When not being admonished by Charles's lurking shadow, Stella would stomp her feet in disgust and mouth but never utter, "Don't this. Don't that. Don't, don't, don't. All I hear are don'ts. Damn those don'ts."

Even when life afforded her adequate sustenance, she was unable to escape the perceived irons of servitude. She was a wanton slave to poverty, a surrendered vassal to a coarsely compassionate yet unyielding spouse, and now an obligate custodian of a child for whom she fashioned love without foundation. Forever adulterated, she was lost and would never understand why. And so she became an unintended juggernaut to the unassuming adolescent of whom she was in charge.

Over the ensuing years, her unconventional obligation did transform into a genuine love for her son. Yet this love wasn't without its imperfections, as the anointed child would be pummeled as a sounding board, a cushion to help ameliorate the contempt and loathing for her spouse.

Afternoon gatherings at Aston Park served as clemency for Stella as she sought to distance herself from Charles. The tribulations of being a muffled and guardedly despondent wife came hand in hand with motherhood. Self-castigating, she would sit and observe the other women, perceiving them to be exaggerating the fabric of their lives.

They were different. She was different, and she knew it. They were certainly more elegant than she. Their dresses were crisp, their nylons were sheer, and their noses were high. They carried themselves with confidence and were of more substantial means.

Enveloped by self-flagellating submission, clearly misinterpreting their attitude, Stella fostered disdain. She uttered her recurring refrain, "Rich bitches—all of 'em," under muted breath as she kept her head down, rolled her eyes, and observed their every move. She seemed to find comfort in creating her own intrinsic affectation of lowliness and self-abasement. It was a comfort zone, perhaps—an abiding theme, to be sure.

Enslaved by and melded to the past, her thoughts served as a tenable foundation for her incomprehensible world. She was obsessively bound to her childhood. She and her cousin Maude would pull or carry a rusted wagon to the poorhouse store, where those on relief would pick through day-old bread and vegetables beyond their prime. Both wearing threadbare flour-sack dresses and scuffed shoes, the girls were held captive by the Great Depression.

"Stella, it's your turn to push—it hurts my back."

Stella was usually at the back of the wagon, lifting, while Maude pulled the handle and barked out high-pitched orders.

"You hafta listen!" Maude would say as she backstepped up the hill. It was a barbed directive from a domineering cousin. As if spat upon from the very beginning, young Stella was a whipping post.

And now as an adult, she was still a whipping post. *You hafta listen*—the command hadn't changed, though its timbre had.

As an attempt to justify her plight, Stella isolated herself by choice. She perceived herself as asocial. In actuality, she was merely ill at ease with new encounters. Being with people was not what stoked her angst; simply meeting them was. It made her feel mired in the muck of uncertainty.

Unable to extract herself from a subsistent past, she found solace in demeaning herself, even when addressed with regard. Confronted with a "Hello, Mrs. Garrett. You look so nice today," she would look away and mutter, "Yeah, right." She'd mutate the remark, assuming it meant that she *didn't* look good on other days. Her waning affect was perceived as polite shyness rather than camouflaged distain.

Once released from the formality of introductions, however, she would become affable, congenial, and unobtrusively outgoing, always appropriate to the setting. Those in her company viewed her as overtly pleasant. People liked her. She was quite attractive and carried herself with a simplistic demureness, of which she was no doubt unaware. She remained an enigma unto herself.

From her perspective, she felt looked down upon—subservient. She would push her outstretched hand, palm flat, into Charles's face.

"See these fingers? Five! I have only five 'friends.' Actually, not even . . ." She'd glare directly into his face. "Not even five. All because of you. Perfect, perfect—always perfect."

Even the dregs of poverty establish a comfort zone. Escape is impossible for some. Walking her child to the park was Stella's apathetic attempt at escape while still confined within prison walls.

When entering the park one day, she offered the same compulsory utterance she repeated every day: "Little Captain, Noah, my dear—don't stray. Stay close and watch the monkeys." Hearing it come from her own mouth made it tangible and sufficient validation of her responsibility. She then looked around to see if others were listening, and she watched to see if they performed similarly with their children.

Under his mother's obligate eye, the Little Captain was not allowed to romp or play in the park. Running freely was taboo, too dangerous. He did, however, find great satisfaction watching primates swing through the artificial trees in Monkey Island. The two-story enclosure was home to white-faced capuchin monkeys.

Sitting pert and straight on the front bench, the little boy, Noah, without realizing it, smiled and glistened as he watched the monkeys freely swing from limb to limb, hand over hand. Vicariously, side by side with his stalwart primate friends, the Little Captain emanated unfettered glee as they twirled and swung through the trees. The monkeys exuded a sense of freedom and assuredness. Even as infants, most never missed their intended mark.

Coddling her loneliness, Stella was unaware of the smile on her son's face. The captive of her own delusional thoughts, she sat pondering, running weary fingers aimlessly along the hem of her flowered dress.

With measured practice, she could banish all thoughts of Charles. Still, she could not escape nor repress her real nemesis, the incessant commands: "Stella, he's our Little Captain." "Stella, if we teach him well, he'll be strong. No limits for him." "Stella, don't forget: no limits"—an insightful pause—"for him." When she looked at the little boy, she saw Charles. And she saw herself as but a governess on the ark.

She stood up, puffed her cheeks, and shook her head with annoyance.

Suddenly, as if enlightened, Noah looked up and began pulling on his mother's dress in an effusive gesture to gain her attention.

"Momma, Daddy told me about the monkeys."

"What is it now?" she demanded with chagrin.

The boy momentarily cowered. His revelation muted, he looked down and placed his hand over his mouth. He grasped her dress more tightly as he pressed his forehead into her thigh.

After a moment, he pointed toward the cage with his arm outstretched. "Daddy told me 'bout that one," he said, his delivery now a reluctant whisper. "The crooked one all by itself in the corner. Daddy said he missed a branch and broke his bones. Daddy said he got broke up because he wasn't good enough. He said people are like monkeys. If they aren't perfect, they hafta pay." He looked up. "Do you know what that means?"

She rolled her eyes while rocking her head. "Yes, little guy." Then she tucked her chin to conceal a whisper: "I sure as hell—" But she stopped short, invoking propriety, lest that word be repeated and come back to haunt her. "I sure as heck—I said, *heck*—do. It means that when you're not perfect, someone always pays."

Her teeth now clenched, with undulating jaw muscles, she mumbled "4-F" under her breath.

Noah resumed watching the monkeys frolic in their enclosure. He divulged only a subtle grin or tempered laugh, cautiously avoiding being overly exuberant, as such a gesture might not be in keeping with his mother's current state of mind. Even being inconsistent in his temperament could lead to his mother's melancholy, casting her into a recurring depression. It would be years before the captain would acquire an understanding of her affliction.

Charles, subject to the same rigors of the Great Depression, occupied a different rung on life's transition from poverty. His pastoral parents experienced lifestyles overseen only by the Sabbath, torrential rains, and the dark of night. With generations of unyielding parents, his lineage was preordained, defined by an indelible template. For the Little Captain, the inherent torch had been passed and the bequeathed compass was true. His course was set.

In preparation for better tomorrows, the always-enterprising Charles remained driven, even when it meant spending sleepless nights paging through used books and attending night classes at the local teachers' college. His wartime civil service designation didn't indemnify him from his inability to serve. Wife and child remained tethered to his burden.

Grim persistence fortified his personal escape from poverty. With a perpetually furrowed brow and prematurely graying hair, he was a man unrestrained, burning the candle at both ends.

None of this could, however, separate him from the son he would mold into perfection. The Little Captain watched, listened, and learned. Stubbornly idealistic, Charles refused to stagnate and become bound to oppressive reality. For Charles, reality and idealism were as bookends, made meaningful only when clarified by time and a transition of events. The Little Captain learned. Regimented in every facet of life, Charles defined the boundaries for both himself and his family.

Noah was unfettered yet stoked by this paternal piety wrapped in perfection. It served the Little Captain well. Nevertheless, having discordant parents infused Noah with words of encouragement intertwined with censure. It was a double-edged sword as well as the lattice upon which Noah would build a foundation.

When his family eventually moved to a secluded farm his father rented at low cost from an inattentive landlord, Noah's separation from his peers was not without effect.

Social skills and worldly precepts eluded Noah's most malleable years.

The requisite loneliness of isolation was, however, supplanted by an uncanny desire to read. Books were portals but also protective and therapeutic shields. Noah saw how his otherwise-foundering mother would lie for hours on a sofa as she chewed her fingernails, book in hand. The feel and smell of a newly opened hardcover gave Noah both comfort and solace. Although his parents provided little sense of harmony, he learned there was a certain accord to be found in the written word.

Noah spent hours reading. Even at a young age, he was captivated by American history and the idealistic acumen and insight the country's founding fathers projected. The classics, which bled pathos, made visible an ingredient not unfamiliar to his personal condition. With the comforts of his literary bond, he no longer felt alone and could visualize his ideal self-image in a perfect, pristine world. With a book in hand, he too could lie for hours, alternately scanning the pages and gazing at the ceiling as he projected himself into another place and another time.

He learned to see life from two perspectives, both extracted from prose. Fiction—life as it actually is. Truth unblemished by bias and prejudicial expression. Nonfiction—personal observation scored with bias and prejudice. Both literary contrivances were self-serving and ideologically satisfying, with nonfiction reconfigured for survival or personal gain. In time, Noah would learn we are all subject to see that which we choose to see, rather than that which actually is.

He learned that both realism and idealism could be framed within the same construct. Mired in reality, the only result was apathy or anguish, and when unchained, anger and chaos. Fiction, the way he wished for life to be. It was real without fear of reprisal. It was not distorted by self-deceiving untruths of a distorted world.

In time, he would put this into perspective, understanding that idealism is what moves the world, but only when juxtaposed with realism or an intellectual understanding of the conditions at hand. Idealism needs a starting point—reality. Idealism sets visionaries' goals in life, while realism tends to entrench stagnation, keeping an advancing world at bay.

The world that confronted Noah every day could only be made better by his idealistic vision of tomorrow. But if perfections were violated and reality were sustained, the results would be deadly.

Summer days were also to his liking, as he became self-absorbed, collecting and corralling frogs and toads behind meticulously molded pebble-and-stick fences. He was in control. The Little Captain learned to love his amphibian creatures by day, and he became entertained and spooked by literary goblins by night. Imagination has no bounds with a little boy at the helm. His childhood experiences would never fade and would serve him well. He gained a keen eye for both flora and fauna, and little did he realize his farm experience would not go without application.

For Noah, being a country kid living in a dilapidated farmhouse wasn't without consequence. He liked people, yet he spent most of his time alone. This disparity proved to be a lifelong encumbrance, for it carried the price of an uncompromising perception of the world. He was the product of two parents, after all—not one.

Chapter Three

*The tinder of one's soul smolders from the fomentations
of the past. Embryonic embers, be they depraved
or virtuous, will ignite. No one can escape their
beginnings. Dire or auspicious, the die is cast.*

HE MAY HAVE BEEN CONCEIVED BETWEEN cardboard boxes
on a hillside, alongside a corrugated metal hovel, or perhaps behind a fish house a distance from Ipanema. It really
didn't matter. The stench of a Rio de Janeiro favela, tempered by hot days and humid nights, permeated the very
marrow of what was to become Caubi Tomayo.

His paternal surname was unknown, without consequence. His mother, Theresa, gave him her surname,
Tomayo—an appellation of her ancestral heritage. Caubi, the
name of a generous former suitor, was simply an afterthought.
Caubi Tomayo came with no distinguished pedigree, yet he
did possess one affectation that spares no man: want.

An antiquated shanty on a squalid hillside served as Caubi's birthplace. A cockeyed doorjamb led immediately into what Theresa described as her "receiving room"—objectified terminology, as if an epithet would elevate her status. Dreary and ill kept, this domicile nonetheless served its purpose.

Flickering aromatic candles strategically placed about the room cast seductive, wavering shadows along the spackled walls. The candles were functional both to entice wanton passersby as well as to ward off the pervasive stench.

Prohibitively small and dank, the room was embellished by a single velvet picture of a jousting horseman parleying with an Andalusian windmill. Theresa thought it added a European flair. The contradictory motif was made complete by a slickened dirt floor partly covered by a multicolored Parisian rug. Two wooden high-backed chairs, a three-tiered chest, and a rectangular table were overshadowed by a strategically placed nineteenth-century Portuguese four-poster bed. At night, Caubi, lacking a crib, would be unobtrusively tucked into the bottom drawer of the chest, where he would be lulled to sleep by complacent moans and the rhythmic squeaking of bedsprings.

Theresa Ruda Tomayo Fundo was the product of a most contemptuous side of Brazilian society. At that juncture in the formative stages of the now-great South American nation, children of poverty frequently became no more than chattel. Rogue police and self-anointed vigilantes sought to cleanse Brazil of its child indigents in an attempt to mitigate a societal stigma. Children without temper of mind or salacious proclivity were as fodder, slaughtered without reprieve.

Transitioning from the safety of childhood to adolescence was fraught with peril. Physically precocious, Theresa was spared the death squads. As a commodity, she could easily blend into the cover of night. Others less endowed would become the killables.

Although thousands perished, Theresa Ruda Tomayo Fundo sashayed without fear as she maneuvered through her terrain. Her dresses were floral and sequined, and they boasted revealing, come-hither necklines—honey for the bees. She spent some of her days and most nights recumbent, collecting cruzeiro to quell her habit and, with irascible indignation, feed her child.

As an emaciated adolescent, Caubi was served up as a prop sitting on a curb, tin cup between his knees, begging for coins from dandies who strayed from Ipanema. During his most malleable years, he was a silent witness to everything abject, learning contempt and survival at a young age. His world was replete with mentors, abject as they were.

Mother and child, victims both, harbored disdain for everything societal. The child, once untarnished with all the beauty of a newborn, would ferment as he came of age. He grew to be jaded and impervious to all things beneficent. Contemptuous, Caubi took heed of the glazed dandies with their baubles and fancy shoes.

Burgeoning as a great nation, Brazil was enhanced by the riches of war and a puree of cultures. Yet with all the naivete of its own adolescence, it too was scarred by discontent. Caubi and the dark side of Brazil were symbiotic. As if willfully strapped to a rail, his course was set.

On a good day, he might receive sweet chocolates from one of Theresa's suitors. Fashionable brigadeiros were tasty and as close as he came to the virtues of milk. He would lick the sweetened milk and cocoa filling from his fingers and suck it from beneath his soiled nails.

Rio was favored by worldly braggadocios whose language was not limited to Portuguese, Spanish, or English but enhanced by French, Italian, and even creolized Papiamento dappled with Dutch. Caubi bore a supple ear and a clever mind, becoming worldly in his own backyard.

Attempting to satisfy a maternal obligation and temper her underlying guilt, Theresa would on occasion supplement her periodic kindness by allowing Caubi to keep a few coins collected at his curbside post. But she would never know that the mere thought of her brought a sinister tightening to Caubi's upper lip.

Even as an adolescent, Caubi became adept at honing flunkies to do his bidding. It was clear that numerous cups held between the numerous knees of his deluded followers would be more lucrative. He operated as sole proprietor, skimming the lion's share.

In time, he realized cunning was not innate but learned. His guile was braced by flowing ebony hair coiffed with confidence. With a contemptuous cant of his head, a subliminal smile, and an air for the aloof, Caubi garnered both pity and specious respect, even at a young age. He played it to his advantage. Subordinates viewed him as one to emulate, attempting to adopt his style and swagger. In lockstep, they gathered as harvested pawns. He called the cadence; they followed.

As he grew, he learned his shantytown possessed more than one lascivious flower to pluck. Tin cups were soon replaced. *Procurement* became his mantra. He was a pimp, and there was no one to disappoint.

On his turf, there were two components requisite for fulfillment. The first was pretense. And the second, money—everyone's nemesis. The first he acquired by observation, and the second by an insatiable thirst—want, satisfied at any cost.

A fedora turned up on one side became his moniker, a diadem that came with a price. Costume jewelry was replaced by the genuine article. Caubi Tomayo, adorned with overlapping chains and sparkling rings, was a pompous man of the town. Jewels, just one insatiable fetish.

On what would prove a momentous occasion, a police officer—one of his mother's frequent tricks—failed to pay. Earlier in the day, the officer had been brandishing a presumptuous stone on his ring finger. He boasted of his alluvial diamond, sifted from an obscure rivulet of the Rio Negro. His bravado had not fallen on deaf ears. He was later found mumbling and bloodied, wandering aimlessly near a local landfill. His ring finger was missing. As was his tongue.

Having crossed an indelicate line, Caubi's transgression proved a faux pas, making him a wanted man. His fate, tenuous in the favela, required a move. The back rooms of Rio beckoned.

Caubi was captivated by something more auspicious than prostitution—an opportunity that would prove more lucrative. Brazil, with its sweeping green, had soil for more than manioc plants and rubber trees. "Happy dust" could thrive there, camouflaged beneath a never-ending canopy of green.

And so the lackeys, loins inflamed, would gather to hear Caubi's enticements of offerings to behold—comely and ripe, previously untouched. But then he would entice them with another type of offering, one all comers clawed and cried for. Nose candy. The followers were transfixed by Caubi's promises to satisfy their greatest craving, which even surpassed carnal gratification.

Coddling malicious reminiscence, Caubi extended his hand toward the sun. With a dexterous thumb, he fondled the ring no longer of use to a blubbering four-fingered man. By intent, he directed a muted sinister smile toward each of his plebs. His onlookers were mesmerized.

"Gentlemen, do you see how this stone glimmers? It becomes even brighter when magnified with a touch of blow—that is, after you've fulfilled your most basic needs."

Caubi once again tempered his smile while gratuitously tipping his hat to his gathered minions. They followed every word, placing their preferred interpretations between the lines.

"I have plans," he told them. "And you, as my subjects, can follow me."

"Like disciples," blurted one of his toadies from the back row.

With a snicker and fingers crossed on the hand behind his back, he pointed up at *Cristo Redentor*, Christ the Redeemer, towering high above the city.

"Not exactly."

His followers, heretics all, were silent, confused.

Caubi threw his head back and laughed. "He may not approve," he clarified. "I have things to do."

On cue, everyone chuckled. Putty in the palm of his hand.

Deluded by hubris and boasting of how he had acquired the ring, Caubi soon needed to be on the move. The cloak of Rio was no longer his protector.

As it had for so many before him, the mighty river would serve as his conduit to safety. By embarking from Belém, the established gateway to the Amazon, he could blend with the metropolitan mix or with the outlying native *caboclos*. As a chameleon under threat, he could conceal his swagger and cower into the night. Feral, he knew when it was once again time to move.

Watching ships navigate the river at a pier-side restaurant, Caubi Tomayo sat with outstretched legs, ankles crossed, waggling a toothpick between his lips. On this waterway, vessels from afar bore myriad flags as they jockeyed their way through the port. Longshoremen unloaded canisters, the contents of which they knew not. Profit, not discretion, was their mainstay.

Caubi's mind was supple as he perused the past and contemplated the future. In silent rehearsal, he began pacing the wharf as he mouthed phrases, deciding how best to manipulate those not yet in his thrall.

He stroked the purloined diamond, removed the tooth-pick while puckering his lips, and feigned a kiss over his acquisition. If there was one such diamond plucked from a rivulet, there could be others. In his pocket, a twig from *Erythroxylum*, the coca plant—a second and more tantalizing option. And heading upriver would bring separation from his past and distance from his pursuers.

Canisters ready for loading lined the pier, their destinations painted in large block letters. Smaller ships found their destinations as far upriver as Iquitos in Peru. Larger vessels were heading for Manaus and beyond on the Rio Negro. One such ship caught Caubi's attention. Its crew members appeared choreographed and agile as they repeatedly looked upward to receive instructions from an overseer positioned high above the landing.

Arms crossed, Captain Helmut Richter stood on the flying bridge and observed a lone man meandering the pier. He categorized the wayfarer as an indigent. There was always use for the impoverished. A beckoning wave was all it took.

Caubi ascended the gangplank as an initial step into a new life. Coming down to meet him, the stalwart captain descended the stairs stiff-kneed, throwing his feet out and clicking his heels. Richter stepped forward, striking a fabricated pose as he extended an enthusiastic hand.

"Velcome aboart. Can I assist, *mein* lowly *Freund?*"

Looking down while extending a flaccid hand, Caubi's countenance was purposefully deferential.

"Yes. You have a nice boat."

The captain leaned forward and placed his mouth against Caubi's ear while coarsely massaging the newcomer's shoulder with his hand.

"Mein Freund," he said with an impassioned whisper, "zis is not *ein Boot*." Standing back while sweeping an outstretched arm in an arc, he continued. "Look. *Sehen Sie— das ist* ein *Schiff. Das ist* mein *Schiff.*"

It wasn't difficult for Caubi to understand. This was not a boat. It was a ship. His ship. A communiqué delivered with the stench of tobacco and a sultry breath.

Disheveled, with wide-set yellowed teeth and using fractured German and English, the skipper wore a frock coat and a senior officer's visor cap embellished with a frayed golden cord—a traditional Kriegsmarine ensemble prior to 1945. One in a long line of German colonists, his lineage was spurious at best. He claimed his ancestors were immigrants to Brazil, initially settling in Rio de Janeiro along with others from the homeland. His time of disembarkation was suspect.

"Lookink for passage?" he asked Caubi. "Vee can use help."

Like an auger, his hand gripped and twisted Caubi's shoulder, following it with a pat. It was confirmation enough. An agreement had been reached.

Little did Richter realize the facade. He was the patsy, not his unsuspecting passenger.

With rivets replaced by expandable wooden pegs, the renovated Liberty ship *Fuga* was compromised in some ways. Nevertheless, it was ample as its new patron forged his way west along the Amazon River, which in some areas resembled a veritable inland sea. Having once transported cargo for the war effort, the ship was now laden with requisite paraphernalia for the manufacture of everything from motorcycles to television sets.

For hundreds of large companies, Manaus's status as a free-trade zone had its advantages. It also brought thousands of people to a part of the world where "free trade" carried a different connotation. The harbor's nooks and crannies, elusive to prying eyes, carried merchandise not included on the captain's bill of lading.

As a first-time passenger, Caubi Tomayo found the voyage productive. It would not be his last. He was selectively antisocial, with his berth located belowdecks. It was a suitable accommodation in which to design a new course. Caubi pondered his fate, which was materializing yet lacking substance.

During the passage, Caubi and Richter skillfully assessed each other, knowing there was proper use for any man, especially if categorized in the ranks of vulnerable servitude. They found themselves playing similar roles, each ingenious and cunning. Both remained attentive, lest they disclose anything that might reveal a veiled character.

Never specifically addressed, theirs was to become a parasitic yet symbiotic relationship. Their burgeoning alliance, embellished with a shroud of subtleties, found them on the same page. The days proved lucrative, in mind and purpose, for the two men.

Their journey had just begun.

As they neared their destination, the ever-changing river took on a unique appearance in the early-morning sun.

Running in parallel, the portside of the river was brown, while the starboard was black as coal. The river was a singular body yet dimorphic, as was its most calculating and ambitious passenger.

At journey's end, the *Fuga* was discreetly berthed on the periphery of what proved to be a thriving harbor. On the hillside, a large flowered mosaic made it clear: this was Manaus.

Caubi watched as the portside was secured. Longshoremen began unloading the vessel while the captain directed shoreline subordinates to the stern, where a gin pole had been jury-rigged to off-load intact boxes of cargo that had been conveniently cradled in broken stowage. The entire event, furtive in its execution, took no more than twenty minutes. Cuban cigars, champagne, and caviar—all in demand when distributed appropriately, and all proving lucrative.

Richter, with a nod of satisfaction, returned to the aft cabin, where Caubi stood watching the process unfold before his eyes.

"For a landlubber, Herr Tomayo, you seem to take great interest in zee affairs of mein Schiff," Richter growled, scowling.

Caubi's indifferent, blank stare expressed a carefully crafted naivete, a cover so as not to reveal a vested interest in the captain's affairs. With confidence, chin jutting out and nose elevated, he simply smiled.

"Yes. I like watching. I learn from watching. I learn from listening too. Why did you order the stevedore into the cowl when we began off-loading?"

Shaking his head and frowning, the captain answered, "*Vee* vere off-loadink? *Nein, I* vas off-loadink. Zee shtevedore is new and must learn zee proper routine for dispatching certain cargo from mein vessel. You shouldn't ask too many questions. Be grateful for your passage."

"Thank you, Captain Richter, sir. I appreciate what you've done for me. I trust our paths will cross again. Agree?"

Clearly weighing his options—and not attempting to hide an attenuated smile—the captain raised his brow, pooched his lips, and slowly rocked his head. "I untershtant. You see, I haff gone srough your belonginks. I know vat you carry in your pocket. There's alvays room for storage and transport on mein Schiff."

Before departing the ship, Caubi turned abruptly with eyes fixed on the captain's. Caubi eagerly shook Richter's hand. The authority was his. With a defiant and insolent air, the swagger was back.

Chapter Four

The high diver has no midway alternative once he leaves the platform. His destination will always be the water.

ON THE DAY NOAH LEFT HIS Minnesota home, Charles mustered strength, with chin up and quivering lips, to fight back a single tear. Taking a labored breath, he handed the Little Captain a leather suitcase and pointed to the monogram NG etched onto the metal clasp.

"For you, my bo—" He caught himself. "My man."

Wearing her finest flowered dress, Stella stood back, diminutive. Her arms extended rigidly downward; her hands clasped tightly to her body below her waist. With no eye contact, she wept silently, choking out an almost inaudible "Goodbye."

Conditioned and transformed by circumstance, Noah assumed his new role as if stricken. Looking authoritatively at his father, he stepped forward and offered his hand.

"Thank you, sir."

Simple, direct, and concise. Charles knew his Little Captain had arrived.

He turned to his mother. "Mom, you did good. Really good. Don't worry—I know what I have to do." Tilting his head with a fawning smile, he gently tweaked her chin. "I won't step in any more puddles."

For the first time ever, he kissed her on the cheek. A true understanding of his mother would come to a conscious level years later.

There were no parting hugs. Noah took a deep breath, turned, and never looked back. Charles, accentuating resolve, nodded his approval with clenched teeth, then quickly turned away. Stella wept.

From the beginning, Noah Garrett's goal was to become a neurosurgeon—for him, the pinnacle of medicine. That perception would never change.

In all his hours of reading, he had discovered how the art and science of medicine had evolved from Galen and Hippocrates to the introspective Wilder Penfield and the genius of Sir William Osler or Harvey Cushing. It became clear to Noah that only from the brain does consciousness—that indefinable, elusive entity—emerge as joy, love, sorrow, and ecstasy, in addition to the merciless afflictions of Pandora's box. His chosen profession left him with no alternatives. For him, any deviation was compromise for naught.

Boston provided all he needed. For Noah, a four-year undergraduate program completed in three years, followed by med school, was a flicker in time. His fate never seemed superfluous nor contrived, but rather preordained and concise.

Less than one week into his residency, he found himself in the operating room's third tier, the back row. Noah was simply an observer, no hands-on. He watched the department chief, the renowned C. J. Baker, who had a reputation for being pretentious and caustically demanding. In fact, he was known as "Barking Baker," or B. B. He was unaware of his moniker. Or if he was aware, it didn't matter to him; it only substantiated his superiority. As skilled as the chief was, Noah presumed his demeanor was likely due to some deep-seated insecurity. By now, Noah knew even people of renown could be shackled by chains from their past.

In addition to the chief, there was Badger, Noah's immediate superior. Dr. Steven Potts had earned his nickname as a transplant from what he heralded as the great state of Wisconsin. Also present were an anesthesiologist; an anesthesia resident; a circulating nurse; two scrub techs; and Noah, the eager beginner on his toes trying to see the procedure in progress.

Standing high on elevating blocks was Baker's lead tech, his private scrub by day and graduate student by night. She and Baker were so in sync that he would simply raise his hand and the appropriate surgical instrument would be there. Not a word was spoken. It was dichotomous how a man of such renown could be so abrasive to everyone around him, save this one technician.

All Noah could see of the gowned woman beneath her bouffant-style cap, worn low over her brow, was a mask and her vivacious blue-green eyes. Diminutive in stature, she nevertheless had a commanding presence. On one occasion, she appeared to look down at Noah and give him a furtive wink. Even if this were mistaken as a dalliance, it did at least ease the moment.

On the operating table was an anesthetized young woman. Ravaged by epileptic fits that were always preceded by garbled speech and followed by a grand mal seizure, she would become unconscious. She was found to have an arteriovenous malformation, a tangle of blood vessels in the left temporal lobe of her brain.

Although she certainly was not an inanimate object, Noah would learn to separate himself from the emotional component of his profession so as not to taint critical judgment—precision fortified by perfection was paramount. Observations at Monkey Island had taught him that invaluable lesson.

Weeks passed. The majority of Noah's days were spent in the OR or examining patients at the nearby clinic—"the Mecca"—which had earned its place in American medical history. His daily routine began by prerounding on all patients—seeing each patient and becoming current on their status—before meeting B. B. for breakfast. Noah always stepped back when B. B. was near. Wide-eyed, Noah was always listening and attentive, just as it had been for the little boy at Monkey Island. When in the OR, however, Noah could hide a grin behind his surgical mask as he vicariously placed B. B. in the cage. A concealed remnant of a childhood past.

At six o'clock each evening, Noah and the other neuro-surgery residents would meet in the cafeteria for dinner, a reprieve frequently cut short by the incessant overhead paging system. Each resident had an assigned number; if called, dinner was over.

For the residents, theirs was a commitment to render their patients the most honest feeling of well-being possible. "First do no harm" was their axiom, and for Noah, an honest man, it was an imperative. It was his sacrosanct belief that life was sacred, and he knew this creed was inviolate. His unbreakable sinew was being fortified.

While having dinner, Noah and his colleagues would observe the change of shift through a row of windows—in particular, they watched the nurses making their exit from the hospital. Noah began looking for one nurse in particular. She was blond and attractive and walked with a fluid gait. On occasion, she would glance into the cafeteria and seem to smile as she left the building.

"There she goes again," said Badger.

Most of the residents were married to spouses they rarely saw by the light of day. Noah, being unmarried, had developed an infatuation for this passerby, so he bore the brunt of their buffoonery. Razzing his fellow residents, especially those his junior, lightened the weight and kept Badger's underlings on an even keel.

Badger, prodding and overtly jocular, grinned daringly at Noah. "Talk to her. You've been languishing over her for weeks. Don't you think it's about time you at least said hello? You're a chicken."

"I'm no chicken. And I'm not, you know, *languishing*." He delivered this retort with his head down, trying to shield his crimson face. "Another time—tomorrow. Maybe."

The next five days were spent in the hospital, without time for dinner or meeting anyone. Noah wore a shroud of angst; however, the thought of speaking with her remained.

Admissions were nonstop. Noah perceived one peculiar patient as quirky, if not challenging. Neither Badger nor his underlings could explain her delayed postoperative convalescence. Theatrical, she displayed an unusual array of symptoms that Noah thought might represent Munchausen syndrome, a mental disorder in which the patient actually causes the symptoms.

However, it was not the woman's weakness that fanned Noah's aberrant diagnostic flame—it was his. All people are different. Some by nature are theatrical. Some simply take longer to heal. And the combination can become an illegitimate pathway to misdiagnosis. Later, when the woman made a full recovery, it would become clear that Noah was mistaken.

She didn't fit into Noah's preconceived mold, though that shouldn't have implied an illicit facade or a person lacking substance. Rigid and annealed to his personal bias, he would not retain this experience as a lesson.

On the flip side of his cognitive coin, he did, however, remember to position himself in the cafeteria to observe the afternoon shift change. Once again, the day crew was leaving, and like clockwork, there she was. Wearing close-fitting jeans and a cotton blouse open at the neck, with blond hair to her shoulders, she moved with confidence toward the exit. Scanning the cafeteria, she smiled and kept walking.

Noah was as stricken as a moth to a flame yet reluctant nonetheless.

"Come on, you wimp," Potts badgered, living up to his nickname. "You've been checking each other out for weeks. Say something."

Wide eyed and uninhibited from lack of sleep, Noah pursed his lips with a deep exhalation and jumped from the table. Attempting not to appear harried, he walked with guarded haste into the corridor, catching her as she was about to exit the building.

Breathless, he managed, "Excuse me. I've seen you go by the cafeteria before. And . . . well . . . I just wanted to say . . . ah . . . hello. My name is Noah. I'm a neuro resident. I was wondering if you might . . . or would like to get together sometime for maybe a . . . a . . . cup of coffee or possibly a glass of wine . . . or something."

In all his life, he had never concocted a more disjointed, clumsy litany of nonsensical words—all accomplished without taking a single breath. He wasn't one to cuss, but an *Oh, damn* was screaming in the back of his head.

Although they couldn't hear him, Noah's gawking compatriots in the cafeteria could see he was stumbling. They laughed at the display. Badger clenched and pumped his fists as though he and his colleagues had just hit one out of the park. Schadenfreude all the way.

Hesitant and expressing a hint of perplexity, the woman looked at Noah for a long second, then smiled and winked.

His jaw dropped. The wink. The same wink as from those blue-green eyes.

"Oh, for—I mean, you're . . . her!"

Looking up at him with a subtle grin, she tilted her head to one side.

"Name's Jessie. Jessie Waters. And I know you're Dr. Garrett. I've been passing instruments to your boss since you started."

"Of course, you are . . . her. I mean, I know you, but only . . . only your eyes. I didn't know you with your clothes on. I mean—"

Oh, Christ echoed through his head. Now crimson, he thought, *What a fiasco.* He had found himself in awkward places before, but never like this. His mouth and brain were no longer connected.

Impishly biting her lower lip, she stepped back. With her palms up, she looked down, panning over her current attire. "Don't be embarrassed. I know what you mean. And . . . yes, I'd like to get together with you sometime—if ever you can find time away from this hospital."

If limbo was indeed a place, Noah wasn't sure if he was entering or leaving. Nevertheless, Jessie's sense of calm gave him a rational footing. Looking down at her while rubbing the side of his neck, he now smiled—while actually breathing—as he spoke. "I've been on call for a long stretch, but I'm off this Saturday. Maybe? If. . . you're not busy . . . ?"

"Saturday's open. Where would you like to meet?"

Smart, he thought. *She wants to meet me, not have me pick her up. After all, she really doesn't know me outside of the*

OR. For all she knows, I could be a creep. If I were, I wouldn't be the first weirdo to pass through these hallowed halls, even if it is the Mecca.

As discerning as her plan was, it did, however, present a bit of a conundrum for Noah. "I still don't know my way around town," he conceded. "So where would you suggest?"

"Well, there's a band playing the Cape Cod Room at the Bentley this weekend. It's a nice place for drinks and dancing, if you'd like."

Indecisively, he raised one cheek while furrowing his brow. "I really don't dance much . . . ," he said, again on his heels, feeling like a bumpkin. "But that sounds like a swell idea."

"I don't dance much either. But a table away from the floor is a good place to talk and listen to the band. What time is okay for you?"

"Anytime—I mean, after five. I'll be done with rounds by then. Badger will cover the service. B. B. and other mucky-mucks will be off giving a conference in San Francisco, so the schedule will be light for a few days."

At the mention of the department chief's moniker, Jessie held back as silent witness with a negligible cringe. After a moment, though, she said, "Seven or seven thirty will get us a table. If that's all right?"

"Yeah, that'd be great. Seven thirty. I'll meet you at seven thirty at the Cape Cod Room—I mean, on Saturday." Noah had stumbled unawares.

Without a smile, her demeanor tempered, as if giving him a pass. She reached up, tweaked his chin, then walked away.

Even though he agonized over meeting her from the first time he saw her walk down the corridor, he was now relieved she was gone. Outwardly, he stood motionless as he watched her walk away. Internally, he jostled with a sense of accomplishment yet also dread of what he had gotten himself into. Putting his fist to his forehead, he turned and walked away.

She's tough, he thought. *I must be nuts. She's different. Never met anyone like her.*

Expressionless, he returned to the cafeteria, where Badger and his fellow residents sat smirking, eager to expound on the situation.

Badger cocked his head as a Cheshire cat intensely in his element. With one eyebrow raised, feigning a Cary Grant parody, he spewed, "Now, now, now—and just what did she say?"

Feet apart, arms akimbo, and assuredly bobbing his head, Noah said, "Do you know who that was?"

With an expansive grin, Badger continued the parody. "I suppose it was Judy, Judy, Judy."

"You know he never said that 'Judy, Judy, Judy' stuff, right? Get serious. I mean it. Do you guys know who that was—or is?"

Badger, leaving his smile behind, looked sincere. "No, Don Juan—who is it?"

"You've worked in B. B.'s—I mean, Dr. Baker's OR. The eyes standing on the blocks. That's her."

Badger began by shaking his head as a staunch negative, but then he followed it with an enlightened pause.

"You gotta be kidding! That fox walking down the hall every night is Green Eyes?"

"You've got that right. Little Miss Green Eyes herself. And she's not a fox. I mean, she is. But her name's Jessie."

Holding two thumbs up, an eager Rick said, "Jessie what?"

From Noah's perspective, the question seemed a bit too inquisitive, especially coming from Rick, who always touted himself as a ladies' man.

"What do you care?" Noah shot back. Then he stopped. "Darn—she told me her last name, but I forgot. I'll have to ask her again on Saturday. I'm meeting her at the Cape Cod Room."

"What? You're going to meet her? I mean . . . *meet* her?" Badger knew just how to put the emphasis. "You mean, you're not going to pick her up?"

"Yeah. That's exactly right. I'm gonna meet her. She doesn't know me. She doesn't really know any of us. She's playing it safe. She's smart. I'd never want any of you to pick me up for the first time with nobody around," Noah joked. "You'd scare the crap out of me. As a matter of fact, all you slugs would scare the crap out of anyone."

"Okay, Romeo—you've made your point," Badger said, attempting to come off his high horse. "She's playing it cautious. Maybe she is smart. I've heard that besides being a scrub, she's in grad school." He smiled, conciliatory. "Time will tell. Maybe she's the one, Dr. G. But as for now, Casanova, there's work to do. A lot of it. Saturday is another day. For now, this residency owns you."

The one.

Strange how Badger's remarks resonated with Noah, causing a rising shivery sensation with a rippling stir in his temples.

Never before, he thought. *Maybe?*

Chapter Five

Expectations, honed by the past, define one's future.

STANDING IN HIS BOXERS in front of a mirror, an apprehensive Noah Garrett went over his list of to-dos at five thirty in the afternoon. Dark-blue blazer, laid out on the bed. Spotted ascot to match. Starched azure shirt, frayed at the collar but pressed. Wing tip shoes, shined. A map to the Bentley, marked with yellow highlighter, laid on his desk.

No time for dithering came to mind—along with a fleeting thought of his father.

Before the mirror, Noah practiced his opening greeting. He wasn't about to repeat his initial snafu, when he had been tongue-tied in the corridor while Jessie stood smiling and confident. His pantless reflection prompted a spontaneous chuckle, however. His face flushed, even though this was simply a rehearsal.

Noah finalized his attire with repeated glances in the mirror. He followed that by curling a small forelock over his forehead. As an attempt to muster reassurance, he assumed an erect flamenco-like stance, snapping his fingers as he took yet another quantifying gander in the mirror. Primed and ready, he paced while repeatedly glancing at his watch, calculating the precise moment he needed to leave. A learned if not inherent need for perfection was consistent with never being late.

His rusted-out Dodge Dart station wagon wasn't much to look at, yet it was clean and it ran like a top, albeit with black smoke coming out of the tailpipe. He drove around the Bentley several times, waiting for a place to park. Just as he found it, a faded green VW Bug with a dented fender and one headlight pointing upward slipped into the spot.

Noah was primed to throw out a definitive gesture, but then he recognized the driver. Green Eyes. She wasn't about to let a rusted junk heap of a station wagon get in her way.

Finding a parking place across the street, Noah stepped out to see Jessie, arms crossed, leaning against the front fender of the Bug. Blond hair covering her shoulders, a tightly molded black dress worn well above the knee, and stilettos to match—this wasn't the woman he had last seen in the corridor.

Smiling and coy, she watched him cross the street. "Hi. I guess I took your spot."

Witnessing the sight before him, Noah was suddenly speechless. The greeting he had rehearsed was nowhere to be found.

With a coquettish bounce of her hip, Jessie pushed away from the Bug, walking seductively toward him with the disarming signature wink he had seen before.

"Our timing is perfect. Since you haven't been here before, I'll be your escort," she said. "I'd rather go in with you."

Doing a stagger step in the middle of the street, Noah stammered, "You . . . you look different. I mean, you look . . . great."

Looking him up and down with a subtle questioning affect, Jessie replied, "And so do you, Dr. Garrett."

With a come-hither flick of her finger, she took him by the arm, escorting him to the curb. "Catchy," she said. "The kerchief you have around your neck—I like it." This was expressed while giving it a quizzical tug as they proceeded to the Bentley.

"Yeah. As a kid, my father always had me wearing a sailor suit with a scarf. It, well, sort of evolved into this. It's an ascot—something chic in my father's day. But before that, all colonial patriots wore them. I like 'em, and they're comfortable, not like the neckties we're required to wear in the hospital. You *do* like it?" he asked, seeking assurance.

"I do. It's . . . well . . . unique."

Not sure what "unique" was supposed to mean, Noah decided to take it as a compliment.

Passing through the lobby of the Bentley, Jessie folded her arm in his, leading him along a marble corridor to the Cape Cod Room. Tables, mostly occupied, filled the room, which had an elevated stage and a small floor obviously meant for dancing. Alabaster sconces exuded warmth in a setting Noah felt was perfectly designed for a first date.

Jessie led them to a single table for two awkwardly located against the stage and, for Noah, too close to the dance floor. Knowing he was on her turf and out of his element, he let her take the lead as he surreptitiously turned his head, biting the edge of his lower lip as a warm crimson climbed up his neck and soon covered his face.

"Gets crowded with this group," said their waiter, who was weaving his way between tables, pen and pad in hand. "Cocktails?" he asked Noah.

Taken by surprise, Noah once again found himself stumbling for a response. "Well . . . yeah . . . a Pushkin." He tried not to look like a rube.

"Nice choice. Interesting," said the waiter. "And for the lady?"

Quick to intercede, Jessie answered for herself. "I'll have a vodka martini, dirty, up." She looked at Noah and winked. "Dirty—it's about the olive juice. I like olives."

Not knowing how to get started, Noah simply sat and scanned about the room in search of something to say. Then he turned directly to Jessie.

"I've been looking at you for months and didn't know you. Now when I look at you, I feel as though I do—know you, that is. Strange . . ."

He saw that Jessie was not only paying attention but doing so with a welcoming smile. It was comforting for a man vacillating between optimism and trepidation.

"Dr. Garrett, you don't really know me—yet. But I know you, and I know about you. That's because I've watched you in the OR and because I know what Dr. Baker thinks of you. He gave me a heads-up. Says you have good judgment and that you're especially good with your hands. Says you're going to be an excellent neurosurgeon."

Leaning forward, Noah not only liked what he heard but was especially pleased to hear it coming from her. "Thanks for sharing. It's Noah. Call me Noah."

Reaching across the table, she grasped both of his hands. "And you, Noah—call me Jessie."

If there had been barriers to maneuver around or idiosyncrasies to manage, both were being addressed and put to rest with the wink of her eye, the smile on her face, and the simple grasp of his hand. Finding themselves on the same page was a relief for Noah. It was obvious Jessie felt the same.

"Your drinks," the waiter said from above them. He gave Noah an apparently congratulatory thumbs-up before placing the drinks on the table.

Jessie saw the gesture and smiled. This wasn't her first time in the Cape Cod Room.

The band, the Raptors, caught Noah by surprise as they began setting up less than an arm's length away. Sitting next to four black men wearing patent leather shoes, spangles, and black tuxedos left him unsettled.

Saying nothing, he slid his chair away from the stage, repositioning himself next to Jessie. Wide-eyed and shaking his head, Noah puffed his cheeks before letting out a deep and telling breath. He reached for his drink, buying time to compose himself.

With an understanding bob of her head, Jessie acknowledged his discomfort with a pacifying smile. Then she raised her glass.

"Cheers," she said as she tipped her head with a magnetic smile. "We have a lot in common," she continued, watching Noah's reaction to his surroundings.

She learned that as children they were separated only by water, a state line, and green pastures. It would become obvious that they were both defined products from whence they came.

The band eased into a tune, slow and rhythmic, which encouraged both the less adventurous and those in the know to file onto the floor. Now courageous from having downed a Russian philosopher, Noah stood and held out his hand. With a genteel flair, he asked Jessie to dance.

Wearing a questioning smile, Jessie dipped her chin. "Do you *really* know what they're playing?"

"No," he delivered with a hard swallow. "Not . . . really. But I'll give it a try."

Once they were on the floor, however, the music abruptly stopped. Just as abruptly, though, the silence was immediately broken by the reverberating keys of a baby grand.

"This is what I meant," Jessie said.

Instantly, she became one with the music, in sync with the escalating tempo. Noah stood flat-footed, looking. Their debut had become a solo. Jessie owned the floor.

Others took notice as well, stepping back to watch. Men watched Jessie with delight, while some of their partners hid their envy behind glares. Noah glanced about the room with relief. At least no one was looking at him.

He was nevertheless relieved when it was over. Even the band gave her a round of applause as she whisked a thumbs-up curtsy and followed Noah back to their table.

"I thought you said you couldn't dance," Noah murmured as he held out her chair.

Looking over her shoulder, she delivered her reply with what had become her patented wink. "I didn't say I couldn't boogie."

Formalities breached, they danced slowly after dinner, while other couples watched with jealousy and anticipation. Noah had never held anyone so close. Moving across the floor, she had buried her cheek into his chest. Looking up, she passed her fingers across his lips as tears rolled down her cheeks. On her toes, she kissed him on the lips and whispered, "Thank you."

He didn't have to ask her for what. He knew.

With shared provenance, they—a farm girl and an out-of-towner—were stepping from the protective seclusion of the Midwest. They were irregular pieces of a pastoral puzzle, which, when juxtaposed, made for a perfect picture.

Over the ensuing months, which extended into years, they experienced the quiet of Boston's bohemian side as they shared secrets, passions, and dreams. She, a neuroscientist well into her master's program, to be followed by a PhD. And he, a neurosurgeon in his six-year fellowship. Together, they were cast from the same academic mold. Leisure time found them immersed in each other while steeped in love of their country and apple pie. Passion without restraint filled their nights. Anticipation defined their tomorrows.

Their playground was the city in which they lived. Boston—where it all began. Stepping out of the linear confines of the Mecca, they strolled through the area of Boston they had come to call home, extending from "Old Ironsides," berthed at Pier 1, to Harvard Square, across the Charles River. History and academia were shared here.

One afternoon outing found them on the Public Garden Monument Walking Tour. As Noah and Jessie leaned side by side against one of the monuments, they looked different. Facing one another, as if peering into a looking glass, they were the same. They saw everything around them through the same lens.

Jessie reached up, feigning to adjust Noah's collar. As he looked down, she tweaked his nose in a playful gesture.

Bantering as they walked, the two lovers enjoyed a game of scrutinizing strangers, making up stories about who they were and what they might be doing. Imagining the bystanders to be foreigners, thieves, or spies—Sacco and Vanzetti or even the Rosenbergs—the couple spun tales of stolen secrets and heinous crimes. Fun and easy.

Noah and Jessie were possessive of their turf. They had a shared perception of who belonged—and who didn't. Their games, while childish, were screened from the purview of criticism and chiseled by antipathy—acceptable when kept to themselves.

On days such as this, they were within themselves, sharing Milan Kundera's overture to *The Unbearable Lightness of Being*. Hand in hand, assuming a leisurely pace, they watched families arrange wicker baskets on checkered blankets on the common.

"They don't know it," Noah said, nodding toward the picnickers, "but they're eating in a pasture that was once filled with horse crap and cow manure."

Saying nothing, Jessie rubbed his hand, recognizing his quip as an example of his occasionally sordid sense of humor. Changing the tenor of their conversations was one of her many talents. Perceptive and charmingly multifaceted, she could transition at one moment from the coquettish ingenue playing whimsical games to the neuroscientist en route to her doctorate in her life's work. Never intimidated, she could hold her own, be it defending her thesis, championing women's rights, or defying any injustice that might besmirch her fellow humans.

"Okay, my eminent Dr. Noah Garrett—your thoughts? You're looking too serious. What's the plan?"

Yielding to her question, Noah stopped momentarily, then turned and stepped in front of Jessie. Looking down at her diminutive frame, Noah passed his fingers across her cheeks, then drew her close.

With a shared embrace, Noah looked up as if retrieving answers from afar. "I am serious," he said. "Just thinking of how fortunate I am. You know, being here in this city with you. We've come a long way. I knew only your eyes for the first six weeks. I didn't know the rest of you—I mean, the other parts that went with the eyes. I'm talking about . . . the real you. I mean, you really care . . . about us . . . for me."

Stepping back with his arms extended, he firmly grasped her shoulders as if to deliver a lesson. "How incredibly fortunate I am to have found you. And because of that, well, I'm blessed."

Even now, after so much time together, he couldn't quell a blush.

She was about to say how lucky they both were, but she quickly refrained from doing so. She knew he wasn't much for attributing good fortune to luck. From his perspective, good fortune was earned, while luck came simply from the roll of the dice. He credited good fortune to diligence and hard work.

In the case of relationships, however, he knew providence certainly played a role. Equating Jessie with the ethereal, Noah had positioned her in a very majestic place. Unique for her, if not precarious for him.

Teasingly compliant, she tapped her finger to his chest. "Yeah, my man, we worked for this," she said, all the while thinking, *I'm a lucky gal, and I'll take lucky anytime.*

Capping the moment with a capricious but endearing peck on the cheek, she suggested they walk the Freedom Trail before preparing for a night on the town with dining and dancing. The latter would never be Noah's forte. He dipped his chin to conceal a labored swallow.

She never ceased to amaze him. She was unique, keeping him on his toes with his head in the clouds. She came armed with a four-pronged snare: she was beautiful, smart, wise, and completely endearing. Shaking his head, he wondered—not for the first time—how all those qualities could be tucked with perfection into five feet, two inches.

With reminiscence stowed, the couple started at the Union Oyster House, America's oldest restaurant. It was, by tradition, a must. Exhibiting reverence, they stepped into the same oyster bar frequented by Daniel Webster, who was described as a multifaceted man, intellectualizing and sharing conversation with both scoundrels and the well-intentioned men of the day. His favorite libation was said to be a tumbler of brandy with water, and it would be accompanied by a plate of oysters, shucked before his very eyes.

Webster was a man near and dear to Noah's heart, a respect both he and Jessie shared. Part of Noah and Jessie's mutual attraction was not only their off-the-farm simplicity but also their true love of history.

Noah reminded Jessie how he was especially enamored by Webster's insight to herald himself as a Federalist. But Webster was also a lawyer, a fact that added variance to Noah's thoughts about the man. Noah ultimately said he had to cut Webster some slack, knowing that the statesman stood for constitutional law—and knowing there were no ambulances to chase in the early nineteenth century.

Jessie listened as he enthusiastically rambled. She loved it when he expounded on matters of substance, even when stippled with what she called sordid-yet-informed favoritism—a foible he would carry for most of his life.

After sharing his historical sketches and a dozen oysters garnished with a local brew, both were satisfied. They stepped into a sunny day and made their way along the esteemed Freedom Trail. They walked through cemeteries and read toppled headstones. For a respite, they stopped to look up at the bronze of Paul Revere.

"Amazing, wasn't he?" Noah said in awe as he stroked his hand over the marble base of the statue.

They next walked through Revere's home. Noah looked at the small bed and whispered into Jessie's ear.

"Short—about your size. Join me?"

She gave him a not-too-gentle elbow to the ribs.

"Move on, buster." As she walked away, she turned for another look at the bed. "Don't think we could pull it off."

They both laughed.

Finding their way to the Old North Church, then to the Charlestown Bridge, they continued their teasing and jousting until they reached the naval shipyard and the USS *Constitution*. Both agreed this would be a yearly hike while in the city tallying CME credits awarded by the Mecca.

In time, they would continue their Boston experience as a family. They were in love, and they made the most of each day, just as they would relish in their tomorrows.

Escaping their pastoral mold and reaching for excitement, they decided to step out of their everyday milieu, be adventurous, and stay at the Fairmont Copley Plaza. They found it sensual and joyfully risqué to live on the edge.

But first, eating at an Argentine restaurant was on the docket for the evening. With a sense of peaceful solemnity, Noah felt blessed as he held Jessie's hand. He thought of recent events and the times and places from whence they came.

It would seem everything was in order.

Chapter Six

Contrary forces occupy the same time and space.

Immersed in history and gilded in play, Noah and Jessie strolled hand in hand, swinging their arms as dawdling children. An evening of reminiscence would punctuate this as a memorable day. They perused sidewalk menus, contemplating which restaurant to choose.

As planned, they chose Argentine, as the beef was to Noah's liking—dry aged and prime. Although he had distanced himself from utility beef and venison, the taste of tallow lingered.

The afternoon's oysters and beer were mere temptations compared to the indulgences at hand. They were treated to the redolence of South American cuisine, aromatic and enticing. Alfresco dining over checkered linen cloths would embrace the romance in the evening air. Lamps cast tantalizing shadows across the tables, enhancing the serenity of the night.

Stepping into the patio area, they were greeted by a stately waiter carrying a white linen serviette over his arm. Dark wavy hair, a gregarious smile, and a confident gait gave him the look of one seeking a vocation more thespian than utilitarian, appearing as an understudy perched in the wings, soon to be summoned to the Broadway stage. His expression was genteel as he escorted Jessie and Noah to a table neatly positioned to allow privacy while still enabling them to view the other diners. A cascade of red bougainvillea served as a buffer between their Argentine restaurant and the adjoining Brazilian bistro.

"*Boa noite, senhor e senhorita.*"

Taken by surprise, Noah cleared his throat, sneering as he slowly looked up at his host. "I'm sorry, but we're in Boston . . . and we speak English, not Spanish."

Jessie placed a shushing finger to her lips and, through clenched teeth, whispered in no uncertain terms, "Get off your high horse. He's just being friendly."

"I'm sorry, senhor—I mean, sir. You must forgive me. And I was speaking Portuguese, actually. I myself am from Brazil." His retort was adeptly delivered not as a condescending correction but as a clarification accompanied by an accommodating smile. Under the table, though, he tapped an impatient foot.

With a tsk-tsk and a head shake, Noah did all he could to keep himself from being more of an embarrassment than he had already been.

Jessie sighed, surrendering a restrained yet indelicate smile. She knew and loved every facet of this man and would address this blemish another day. She was also amused by the waiter's formality and gave him a wink as an attempt to mend Noah's indiscretion.

Wide-eyed, taking a deep breath, the waiter tilted his head and slowly shrugged while wrangling an expression morphing between a smile and a frown. After Jessie graciously assured him they didn't need his immediate attention, he made his way to the next table.

Noah repositioned their seating arrangement, with Jessie facing the entrance and her back toward the Brazilian restaurant. Superstitious in a jocular sense, she never wanted to be found holding aces and eights with her back to the door. The real reason: she wanted to see what was happening. One of her fanciful quirks Noah found amusing.

As they perused the menu, Noah's attention was drawn to the entrées featuring Argentine beef, which, per the bill of fare, was organically raised and matured to perfection on the majestic Pampas.

"Roaming free makes for succulent and tender meat," he said in a joking tone.

Suppressing a muffled chuckle, Jessie rolled her eyes, nodding approval.

"Yeah, I like the sound of beef," Noah continued. "And you, Jess?"

With a hum, she said, "Nice . . . but I'm up for pheasant."

Tucking her chin toward her chest and smiling coyly, she looked up at Noah.

Noah instantly blushed. He knew what this jab meant.

The couple had recently traveled to Maui for sabbatical. Prior to their departure, Noah had packed two frozen pheasants on ice in his suitcase. They were meant to be a special surprise—a mainland meal on a tropical island. An "exotic" delight in an unlikely locale. However, once in Maui, he discovered the bird was readily available on the island. In fact, there was open season on ringnecks throughout the year.

Well intended, the pheasant incident-turned-debacle was part of Noah's crusade to remain "unique" in her eyes. For her part, Jessie considered it an act of "needing approval."

"I know you want me to tell you once again that your pheasant dinner was not only well thought out but perfect," she teased him lightly, knowing his need for an occasional caress.

"That night we had the pheasants—that's when you told me all about your fascination with Thomas Hardy," Noah reflected. "Remember? I agreed our first son would be named in his honor. Thomas. Thomas Garrett."

"Our lives are better for what we're doing," Jessie said suddenly.

"And what's that?"

"Memories. Making memories."

Holding his hands in hers, she leaned forward and whispered, "That dinner was special. It was meant to please. You won a bit of my heart that night, and you won the rest of it bit by bit until you had it all. Never have any doubts"—she held out her palms, as if making an offering—"it's yours."

For a moment, they simply sat and looked at each other. She leaned forward and pressed her gaze on the man she called her friend, her protector, her lover.

"You know, I love looking into those eyes," Noah said fondly. "Before I met you—I mean, *really* met you—I met your eyes. Do you remember? The first time we really communicated—I mean, without words—was when you winked at me. I was afraid to talk to you. After all, you knew more about an operating room than I did. You were confident and had the department chair, that miserable curmudgeon, in the palm of your hand. He could chew a resident up and spit them out at the drop of a hat. But you, you manipulated that old despot like dough in those pretty little hands. Me, I was a fish out of water. Most people wouldn't know what it's like—that is, meeting someone for the first time in an operating room, covered from head to toe by caps, gowns, and shoe covers. Eyes. All you see is a person's eyes. And yours are the most beautiful eyes I've ever seen. That's all I needed to see."

Reaching forward, stroking his fingers along Jessie's cheek, Noah said, "You do know, eyes are the window to your soul. I'm no bard, that's for sure. But I could see . . . you . . . the real you. From that very moment, through your eyes, I was captured by your soul."

Jessie looked down at the menu, attempting to conceal tears of a dream come true. "You're my poet," she whispered.

Just then, the waiter returned to their table, appearing concerned. "Senhorita, are you all right?" he asked.

Embarrassed, Jessie glanced up at the waiter while blotting her cheeks. "Yes, I'm fine," she said simply. "Joy. Just tears of joy."

The waiter nodded, quickly took their order, then stealthily slipped away, not wishing to impede their intimate moment any further.

Noah reached out once again to touch Jessie's cheek, but raised voices coming from the adjoining Brazilian restaurant made his hand jerk midreach. A loud argument had interrupted the peace of their evening.

Jessie leaned back to investigate the commotion. Noah froze for a moment, taking in this portrait of beauty with her blond hair offset by the cascade of bougainvillea. He then leaned over the table and cupped his hands around his mouth to mute his whisper.

"Can you hear what they're quibbling about?"

Jessie pursed her lips and squinted her eyes as if to enhance her hearing. "No." Mimicking Noah's pose, Jessie now leaned forward and spoke through funneled hands. "But it sounds like more than a quibble."

It made Noah think of the fantasy games they played while watching people at Boston Common. Nose to nose, their querying resembled comedic noir. Jessie's expression wisped into a smile as Noah inconspicuously peered over her shoulder to do some investigating himself.

"What do you see?" Jessie asked, watching Noah watching it all.

Noah craned his neck and bobbed his head in an attempt to peer around and through the floral trellis. He could barely make out the group of men causing the tumult, though two men in particular stood out.

Noah shrugged while holding out empty hands. "I can't see much. Four or five guys at a table. Arms waving. Foreigners. One guy's dark skinned. Dripping in jewelry. Skinny. Almost . . . plastic." Noah was suddenly reminded of an odd knickknack his mother used to keep in a shadowbox on the living room wall. "One's white," he said, continuing. "The skinny dark-skinned guy has a funny hat, turned up on the side. The white guy has a scruffy cap, like a captain would wear."

"What do you think it's about?"

"Not sure, but the skinny guy with his back to us is waving his arms and pointing his finger at a fat guy." He paused for a moment as the argument seemed to reach a new level of intensity. "Now the white guy just stood up. He's banging his fists."

Noah watched and listened as the din on the Brazilian side grew louder. Patrons closest to the disruptive mix began sliding their chairs and tables away from the escalating chaos.

"What's he saying?" Jessie whispered. Keeping her head down in order to grant Noah a better view, she lifted off her chair while leaning over the table on her elbows, keeping her head down.

"Can't tell. Something about 'lubals' and a pigeon."

"'Lubals'? What's 'lubals'?"

"Not a clue. Maybe it's foreign. The white guy sounds like a kraut. You know, German."

To avoid being recognized as a voyeur, which he was, Noah now looked down at the table.

"It's none of our business," he said quickly.

Choking back laughter, Jessie sat down, putting her hand over her mouth. Then she straightened and listened intently, her eyes looking off to the right in concentration.

"Sounds Spanish. Maybe Portuguese. People in Brazil speak Portuguese."

Noah looked up again. "Whatever it is, they're pissed. I mean really pissed. The fat guy just gave the white guy the finger. He's yelling something about an opera."

Just then, the man with the jewels and turned-up hat pounded his fists on the table so loudly that the entire restaurant—both restaurants, actually—were ordered silent. In the momentary void, the bejeweled man slapped the fat man alongside the head, then exploded away from the table.

Noah gaped in confusion as patrons and staff bumped into each other in an attempt to both quell and escape the resumed pandemonium.

"Oh, good. A waiter is finally going over to their table," he said.

Regaining her composure, Jessie rested back comfortably in her chair, as had most of the people in the restaurant.

"Yeah, they're settling down," Noah said. "The waiter is repositioning tables and chairs. And the way he keeps holding his hands together—it looks like he's praying, I think he's trying to apologize to everyone for the ruckus."

"It's about time. That didn't sound good. Creepy."

"I don't know what opera has to do with anything," he said. "I'm no Sherlock Holmes, but they don't look like theater types to me. Just a bunch of goons. Probably drunk. Squabbling over money."

Jessie shook her head, then puckered her lips and leaned seductively over the table. "So, shall we get back to the matter at hand? Shall we talk about our plans for tonight?"

Noah dropped his gaze, biting his lower lip. "Now you're talking."

Sitting upright, Jessie fastened her top button with a provocative smile. "Nasty! I'm talking about *now* tonight."

With a mock frown and a wink, Noah made a low noise. "I understand," he said.

Jessie gave an impish grin and cocked one eyebrow. "My Little Captain is getting bawdy."

"What's the bawdy stuff?"

"For a guy who takes everything so seriously, you have a steamy side. I like it." Elbows on the table, her chin resting in her palms, Jessie continued. "I like that—the seductive stuff. After all, I'm not always a frump in a lab coat. I'm a farm girl. That makes me the farmer's daughter, right? You know what they say about the farmer's daughter. Later tonight you can be the salesman who lost his way and stopped at my farmhouse to ask for directions. Get it?"

"Got it." He blew her a kiss.

The gun's report was sharp. For a split second, life's cinema stopped midframe, only to return to a different feature.

The Brazilian patio erupted with curdling screams. Chairs and tables were overturned. The fat man held his chin, blood gushing from between his fingers, as he ran, choking, from the patio.

The Argentine restaurant was bone-chillingly quiet. Everyone stood, gaping at one table.

Her eyes were open. Her cheek was pressed against the table. Her expression was tranquil, serene. With each heartbeat, blood poured in spurts from her mouth.

Expressionless, Noah slowly rose to his feet. His face as if carved in stone, he looked down at the apocalypse before him. "What? This can't . . . can't . . ."

In that instant, she was gone. Dead.

In disbelief, as if animated in slow motion, he reached forward and passed his fingers through her hair as he stared at a lifeless face. As if restrained by a great pause, there was not a sound to be heard.

Suddenly, like an embittered evangelist, Noah threw his head back, looked up with jaw clenched and teeth bared, and shook his bloodied fists to the heavens. "Damn you! God, damn you!" he screamed. "Why did you do this? Why did you do this to me?" He sank to his knees, foundering in a bottomless abyss, never realizing what he had just said.

In that instant, he became reconfigured. It defined what he had just become—now, who he was.

The bullet had entered the back of her head, exiting her mouth. Her blue-green eyes were still open. The first time he had met her, it was the eyes. Her beautiful eyes.

His grief took form. He chose not to be consoled. The ultimate pain is not physical.

When the police came, he was sitting, inscrutably rocking back and forth, his hands clasped between his knees, condemning the same God he had thanked every night for bringing heaven into what was now a former life.

Chapter Seven

Be it an affliction or a blessing, transformation is
nevertheless a defining process.

THOUGHTS MUDDLED, DR. NOAH GARRETT, the Little
Captain, walked aimlessly along the streets of Boston for
days. With each step, an imperceptible transformation
took place.

Incessantly on his mind, Jessie was a replicating elegy
without an end. Her eyes were reflective and clear, her hair
gossamer as it wisped in the breeze. Every facet of who
she had been was shadowed by despair. Embittered, Noah's
pain, turmoil, and anguish transformed into hatred—
an emotion he had never experienced. But this was now
another man.

He was dying from the inside out. During the day, he
could get lost in his work. But upon returning home, he
found nothing had changed. Going to sleep, he wished he

would never awaken the following day. He always did. The pain didn't stop. It was worse every day.

His options became clear: live or die. Driven by an unyielding sinister force, he chose to live. Resolute and alone, his objective took form. He would start where their lives had ended.

Retribution would be his.

Each morning, he stood, staring beyond his bedroom window, muttering. "Damn you. God damn you—I will find you . . . you miserable bastard. You will pay." It was the lexicon of a man transformed. *Foreign* took on a new and vile meaning.

The police had determined Jessie's death to be a tragic accident. She had not been the intended target. She was simply in the way.

It was obvious the fatal shot had come from the Brazilian bistro and had been fully intended for someone in that restaurant. Flesh and bone fragments defiled the intervening bougainvillea hedge. Likely, the fat man—bloodied, drunk, and awkwardly stumbling from the bistro—was the intended quarry. All the witnesses confirmed that immediately prior to the shot, a man had angrily exited the restaurant. In compliance, they all agreed that man was dark clothed and slender, wearing a fedora with the brim turned up on one side.

Unless new information surfaced, the case was closed. It was as though she had never existed.

Discouraged yet undaunted, Noah dismissed the police's condolences. In fact, they offered nothing: no assistance, no suggestions, no relief.

Weeks passed before he returned to the Argentine restaurant. A sleuth he wasn't. But he assumed that factitious form, retaining the intrepid tenacity he had learned while peering into a monkey cage and beyond. No dilemma or task insurmountable.

In the twilight, he stood curbside, looking across the patio. The tables were positioned just as they had been that evening. Checkered cloths, flowers, candles—all the same, as though nothing had ever happened. Somber, he slowly turned his head while passing tremulous fingers over the menu displayed on the maître d' reservation table.

Why Argentine? Why aces and eights? Why not me?

Noah wrung his hands. Marginally hesitant, he walked slowly to the hedge near the table where they had sat that evening. He saw long flowing hair emblazoned before the cascade of red bougainvillea. Parting the floral divider, he could see the rectangular table on the adjoining patio from which the deadly shot had come.

Walking in his direction, the same young waiter cocked his head, initially trying to place this ashen-faced patron.

"Oh . . . it's you. Senhor, I'm sorry. So sorry."

"Yeah." Unable to quash his anger, he was terse. "Sorry doesn't help." He quickly turned, pointing to a chair. "Sit. Talk to me. I'm trying to figure this out. What's your name? Where ya from? Why are you here?"

Compliant, the waiter sat abruptly. Mouth shown, he shook his head, not knowing where to begin. "*Here*, I'm Christopher. Christopher Martin. My given name is Jesus Garcia. Buenos Aires. I've worked here almost one year. I go to the school for the performing arts during the day and wait tables at night. Others do it too." He spit out the sentences in rapid succession without taking a breath.

So, Noah had been right about the waiter's thespian aspirations. His glare was tempered by a smile, a fleeting slip into the past. Although contorted, it was his first smile since that night. It quickly receded, though.

"Ever seen 'em before? The guys on the Brazil side."

Jesus sat upright, fidgeting as if on a witness stand. "No, sir."

"You know the waiters over there?"

"Of course. Some of us go to the same school."

"You know who was working when she"—he faltered—"that night?"

Jesus's subservient gaze remained fixed to the floor. "Yes. Marco. We still talk about that night."

"Don't be afraid. Just talk to me," Noah said, a little gentler now. "Did Marco know those guys? Did he hear anything?"

"He'd seen them before but doesn't know who they are. They always paid in big bills." He held out his hand, pinching his index finger to his thumb. "*Mas eles deixaram uma gorjeta pequena.*"

"What?"

"Sorry. A small . . . tip," he said, finding the right word. "They always left a very small tip."

"How do I find 'im? Marco, I mean."

Jesus hesitated. "I'll call him now?" It was a question, not a statement. His hands were clasped, timid. "It is okay?"

"Yeah. Call him."

He excused himself, walked to the phone located on the reservation table, and dialed. A few moments later, he said into the phone, "Marco, this is Jesus. I'm talking to the guy whose . . . whose friend . . . was killed. He wants to ask you some questions."

After a quizzical pause, he said his goodbyes, hung up, and looked toward Noah. "He's coming. Now. Can I get you something? Coffee?"

"Yeah. Coffee. I'll wait."

Jesus hurried back with coffee, cream, and sugar served with a napkin on a silver tray. "This is for you. I must attend to other tables," said a bowing Jesus, who, though wishing to please, was noticeably uncomfortable and eager to take his leave of this grieving yet angry shell of a man.

Noah suddenly found himself alone at the fateful table. Eyes glazed, he pondered the room, turning his head slowly from side to side. His lips quivered as he momentarily regressed. Scanning the bougainvillea hedge, Noah could obviously tell that a portion of it had been cut away and replanted.

Fifteen minutes passed before he quickly jerked himself back to reality as a trembling Marco appeared and positioned himself on the very edge of a chair. With his hands folded beneath his chin, as if in prayer, he spoke without looking directly at Noah.

"Sir, I remember you. You want to speak with me?" He expressed the same timidity as Jesus. "But the police already asked me all the questions."

"I'm sure they did."

Noah motioned for Marco to sit. In response, Marco sat back and repositioned his chair a distance from Noah.

"Jesus said you'd seen those guys before."

"They'd been here a few times over the past year. They always sat at the same table, kind of away from everyone else. The closest table was . . . ah . . . well . . .yours." He looked down at the table. "Where we are now."

"You know where they're from?"

"Brazil, I believe. I've heard them speak Portuguese, and they've mentioned São Paulo and Rio. Oh, and one guy is German, I think."

Noah nodded, remembering the one white man among the foreigners. "Did they ever pay with a credit card?" he asked.

"Never. The same guy always paid. The one with the narrow eyes and skinny chin. He wears a black leather jacket and a hat with one side turned up, kind of cool-like. He is easy for me to remember. He reminds me of Jesus. The hair—long, black, wavy like a movie star's."

"You from Brazil?"

"Yeah, Belém. A many-island city on *Amazônia*. Why?"

"Because those guys are Brazilian too, and I'm not sure where to start. There's so much I don't know. We heard them say things we didn't understand." He pointed an accusing finger directly into Marco's face. "*You* have to help me."

The authoritative statement caused the waiter to lean back, yielding and obedient. "I'll try!"

"They used a word that sounded like 'lubals' or 'luvals' . . . something like that. What's it mean? Spanish? Portuguese?"

Marco looked upward while leaning back in his chair. Slowly folding his arms across his chest, he puckered his lips while furrowing his brow as a vain attempt to retrieve an answer.

Finally, he shook his head. "No, senhor. I don't know what that means."

"They talked about opera or going to an opera. Does that mean anything?"

"I don't know about an opera in Boston, but there might be one." Suddenly wide eyed, Marco leaned forward and quickly raised both hands as if stricken by an epiphany. Seeking affirmation, he began rapidly bobbing his head. "You could look it up in the theater section of the newspaper. That might help."

"No. I already checked. There was no opera in Boston. Not at that time," Noah said impatiently. "But they mentioned the opera many times. Said 'always at the opera' and 'it works for the pigeon at the opera.'" He paused and frowned, deep in thought. "You said these guys talked about São Paulo and Rio. Do they have operas in those cities?"

As if teaching a lesson, Marco regained his composure and pointed a chiseling finger toward Noah. "Senhor, Brazil is a very cosmopolitan country. Opera is important. There are beautiful opera houses in many cities: São Paulo, Rio, Manaus—"

"What's that, Manaus?" Noah interrupted.

"Senhor, Manaus is a great city on the river, hundreds of miles from Belém. There you will find the most beautiful Teatro Amazonas, an opera house built long ago. Its history is famous to everyone. You don't even know of it?"

On edge and clearly irritated by what he interpreted as a condescending question, Noah leaned toward Marco while punching his folded fist into an empty hand. "Why should I?"

"Manaus is the largest city in northern Brazil," Marco said. He then turned his head as if eavesdropping on a conversation, only this conversation existed in memory. "Oh yes. The fat man, the one who ran out with the bloody face—he mentioned the Teatro Amazonas more than once. He always spoke loud. I remember the skinny guy with the curved-up hat would scold him for having a loud mouth. The fat guy was always drunk too—even before they came to the restaurant. That made the skinny guy really upset."

Rapt, Noah leaned forward.

"The skinny guy always spoke very quietly," Marco continued. "Even when he ordered his food, I had to ask him to speak louder so I could hear him. He would never look at me when I spoke to him. Like I wasn't important. He was the boss," he said definitively.

"How could you tell?"

"I guess because of the way the other guys looked at him. Mostly they listened. The fat guy—he kept interrupting. The German spoke with his open hands in front of him, like he was holding an invisible bowl or something. He might also have been sort of a boss, because he said a lot too." But then Marco shook his head, disagreeing with himself. "No, the skinny guy—he was the *real* boss. Always in control. But he got really mad that night, though."

Noah nodded. He remembered how the bejeweled man had slammed his fist, slapped the fat man, then stormed out.

"The skinny guy was the first to leave that night," Marco said. "I mean, just before . . . you know . . . it happened. We think he did the shooting, but we're not sure."

Extending an outstretched hand with fingers apart, Noah pointed to one finger at a time, assigning a culprit to each finger. "Okay. Do I have this right? First, the skinny guy spoke quietly, almost too soft to hear, but he was the head guy. Right? Now. Second, the white guy—probably German—was next in charge." Looking squarely at Marco while tapping his ring finger, Noah remained concise. "Third, except for the fat guy, who was generally drunk and loud, the other two guys said nothing. Right?" Noah bobbed his head, seeking affirmation of his interpretation.

"Yeah. They were sort of tagalongs. They hardly talked, but one of them might have said something about a ship. They looked different. They were, well, kinda small."

"Different how?"

"They were short. They looked sort of like Indians. You know, the native people."

With a bit of a snarl, Noah leaned back and threw both hands in the air. "None of this makes sense. Anything else?"

Marco shrugged. "I don't think so."

Shaking his head, Noah stood, casting authority as he again pointed a finger at Marco. "If you or Jesus or anyone else remembers anything, call me. Got it?" Handing Marco his card, he turned to leave.

Almost as an afterthought, Marco took hold of Noah's arm.

"Wait—I remember. The white guy shook his finger at the fat guy and called him '*ein fettes Schwein*.'" Smiling, Marco made it clear he understood some German and could translate what he had heard. "Many Germans came to my country. Understand? After the war."

Irritated and feeling out of the loop, Noah was curt. "No—but thanks," he said.

As he was about to leave, he stopped and, with a querying look on his face, turned back to Marco. He nodded to the card Marco still held in his hand. "If you think of anything else, call me. Because you know things about this Manaus place, and I don't. I might get back to you. Okay?"

Noah didn't wait for a response; he abruptly left.

Returning to his apartment, he cussed under his breath as he sifted through the little information he had. Lying on his bed, he stared at the ceiling.

"Lubals . . . operas . . . Manaus . . . down there," he mumbled.

Somehow it had to make sense; those words had to have some connection or meaning.

"Why'd you do this to me?" he muttered toward the heavens.

Noah was temporarily defeated by the disjointed ambiguity of words. A deep sigh left him exhausted. Running his fingers through his hair, he drifted to sleep amid tapering words: "Time. It'll take time."

Chapter Eight

When intractably fettered to naivete, a commitment,
no matter how forthright or admirable, will always
have the same outcome . . . a price will have to be paid.

LATEX, ONCE MORE PRECIOUS THAN GOLD, exuded from the coveted *Hevea brasiliensis*. With a breath of air, it took on a new life: rubber.

The milky-white sap that oozed from this exceptional tree wasn't collected with ease, however. Lowly trappers traversed large tracts of land only to amass a limited yield. The forest fungus *Microcyclus ulei,* indigenous only to Brazil, ravaged trees growing in close proximity. However, if the trees were carefully grown on plantations, they would be free from the fungus, and production and financial returns could be enormous.

Brazil became inundated as would-be barons rained in, like locusts, from North America and Europe. Brazilian "green gold" was king—that is, until Sir Henry Alexander Wickham, a Londoner, pilfered seventy thousand seeds from the *Hevea* tree. He transported them to Liverpool and then onward to plantations in Sri Lanka, Africa, and beyond, where they would grow unimpeded, fungus-free, as far as the eye could see. This strangled Brazil's rubber industry forever. Brazil's economy and her people were in turmoil, ravaged by the industrialized North and its eastern surrogate, Europe.

Maximally leveraged, Claudio Almeida had acquired vast tracts along the Rio Negro—a prolific rubber haven—before Wickham's theft. Then he found himself plunging from the precipice into the throes of despair. Selling his holdings piecemeal could only marginally keep his creditors at bay. His tenuous circumstance was eventually assumed by his only son, whom he both purposefully and wishfully named Abilio, delineating expertise. While a handsome young man, he was clearly not an expert, so his countrymen simply called him Belo.

A dark side of innate family pride permeated the Almeida clan. Claudio, uneducated, brandished a stern hand as he carved a direction for his son. Incapacitated by anguish, Claudio made clear that Abilio had to preserve and protect all that was theirs. Pressed and destitute, however, Claudio failed to vet potential investors who might guide him through this morass.

Following Claudio's premature demise, reportedly at the hands of an overzealous American entrepreneur, Abilio inherited the remaining land—and with it, a complex mortgage beyond his expertise and ability to pay. A portrait of the sinister gringo was fixed in his mind.

Proud, compromised, and vulnerable, Abilio was the product of a conflicted composition. Living in a country that had plummeted from feast into famine, he had inadvertently inherited not only his father's land but also his plight. It was an incomprehensible burden. Like his father, Abilio found himself deluded by hope, betrayed by deceit, and undermined by the confines of his own despair. Justification for both men's anguish had foundation and history.

In time, the world learned that not only rubber embodied the heart of Amazonia. The lumber barons came next, plundering the land. For Abilio, lessons from the same school of remuneration did not fall on deaf ears.

But no matter the travail, he was made whole by Lucia, his wife of twenty years. She would bring him more than substance and strength as she gave birth to their only child. Lucia, frail and compromised by age, lived just long enough to name the child after Princess Isabel the Redeemer, who had enacted the *Lei Áurea,* the Golden Law, which ended slavery in her beloved country.

As the child grew, she frolicked and played with friends along the garden paths surrounding her pious home. As a babbling child, she fumbled her words, and "Princess Isabella" was transposed into the inerasable moniker "Sabella." Sabella she would forever be to her father, friends, and eventual lovers.

Sabella found joy in traveling with her father along the mighty Rio Negro, which served as a thoroughfare for nomads and the fishermen who provided food for the people of Manaus. Its infinite bounty satisfied the palate. For the romantic at heart, it fortified the legend of boto, the pink dolphin. Everything was beautiful.

The rain forest was her passion. Her unconventional childhood, combined with Brazil's lustrous history, gave her the perception that the country was full of wonders for all to behold. Where she lived was the most perfect place on earth, and Manaus was the only home she had ever known.

She and her father would meander hand in hand through the large expanses of the rain forest still in his possession. He would coddle and teach this child about identity, ownership, and pride. He dressed her as a princess even as they danced through puddles and mimicked monkey sounds, easing their way beneath the never-ending canopy of green.

She also learned of Curupira, the great protector of her land. This mythical boy with flame-colored hair possessed great strength and cunning, which could drive away all who would threaten this extraordinary land. Little did Sabella know it was her destiny to personify this myth of a jungle child whose feet were assembled backward to fool even the shrewdest, most diabolical invaders of Brazil.

Abilio imparted to his daughter his inherent wisdom of the forest. Although timid, he always spoke with fervent reverence as he kneeled in front of her, eye to eye. He shared the names of the abounding flora, including manioc, or sweet cassava, a staple at every table throughout the region. He cautioned her that its liquid supernatant was laden with cyanide and could topple man or beast.

As she grew older, though, she witnessed her father's demeanor change. This change became especially noticeable on one occasion, as they walked past the wondrous Samauma tree, the "Queen of the Forest." This time, he cast his eyes to the ground, as if in two places.

"This is a tree of life," he said simply. "A tree that will enrich your life."

Conflicted, Abilio had but two loves—Sabella and *floresta tropical*, the grandest rain forest in the entire world. Ultimately, he pledged that his daughter would become the first in his family to be educated, not realizing that such a commitment to one love would come with an extraordinary price to the other.

So, Sabella was taught everything from forest management to Greek mythology. The Free University School of Manaus, the first university in Brazil, was more than an institution. It was a fulcrum from which Sabella could forge a career free of want and despair.

A formal education was her ladder for success. But most importantly, she was taught the role she must play, as the expectations had already been scripted by her mother and fulfilled by her father. As a young woman, she assumed a matriarchal position, which her father looked upon with a pride that redefined his qualities as a man.

While attending school, Sabella worked menial jobs and sought boarders in order to feed and clothe her two-person family. More than fortuitously, her pleasant nature eased her into a position at her favorite place in all of Manaus and possibly the entire world—the famous Teatro Amazonas.

Initially crafted from the hubris of rubber barons, this edifice served as a place of parley for tourists, opera aficionados, and all comers. However, Sabella and many of her people shared the same preconceived prejudice toward those alien to Brazil.

Unbeknownst to her, the *teatro* would also serve as the nexus for two men sharing a pivotal moment.

Chapter Nine

If never brought to a conscious level, a whirlpool of ephemeral thoughts will persist as a repository, only to be unexpectedly revived at a later date. Powerful. Real.

CAUBI STEPPED FROM THE GANGPLANK into the bustle of Manaus with a sense of reprieve. Pounding one clenched fist to his chest, he turned for one more look at the *Fuga*. It wouldn't be his last.

Her captain, standing portside, looked down and momentarily extended his right arm in an angular salute before quickly tipping the brim of his cap, bidding farewell. An implied friendship was established. Properly enriched, it could grow.

Caubi returned the gesture with a smile, flicking a quick salute from what would become a telltale trademark fedora. Turning quickly, he looked down and clicked his heels, all the while smiling, as he knew full well to whom he was bidding farewell.

Weaving his way through crowded streets was not an unfamiliar activity. Worldly, he was ready to meet all challenges. Life, after all, was simply a series of conquests, relative experiences, each serving as foundation for the next.

The hillside leading from the water's edge was filled with a clutter of shops hosting assorted curios. There were fragrances ranging from the accumulated acrid mustiness of centuries to the tantalizing aroma of flowers indigenous to the region. Even so, the overwhelming smell of eviscerated fish filled the air. At least some of these familiarities gave him a sense of home. Comfort goes a long way to amplify confidence.

With an air of exaggerated nonchalance and with one hand partly tucked into his pants pocket, Caubi strolled, his strides long and effortless. With his other hand, he gripped a duffel slung over his shoulder, as did others darting along the streets of this city hidden in the clutches of an incomparable sea of green. Being enveloped by a throng of people served Caubi's purpose. A singular tree does not stand out in a forest. Yet by his very nature, he did just that.

Caubi passed through the Nossa Senhora das Graças, the fashionable business district. On the fringe, the boutiques were replaced by modest homes tucked among manicured shrubs and cobblestone walkways.

Catching his eye, a handwritten sign read, *Quarto para Alugar*—Room for rent. The home, humble by its simplicity, brought a smile to his face.

"*Perfeito.*"

Nose up, running his fingers under his chin, he repositioned his hat, tucked in his shirt, and stepped to the door.

A note was appended to the screen: *De volta às cinco horas—* Back at five o'clock.

As an implied right of possession, he sat on the stoop, crossed his legs, leaned against the door, and promptly fell asleep. Rest came easy.

"Senhor. Senhor," came as a whispered but nevertheless intrusive arousal. "Can I help you?"

Emerging from sleep, Caubi looked up, squinting into the sun. Shielding his eyes and craning his neck, he raised his upper lip, attempting to make sense of a blurred silhouette. Leaning to one side, he could see the sheen of onyx hair flowing over copper-toned shoulders. The woman's smile was broad and genuine. Wearing a leopard-print kimono top and fitted jeans, she was both stunning and seductive. She was unintentionally provocative, though; enticement wasn't her intent.

Swatting dusty trousers, he jumped to his feet. Fumbling with his hat, he tried to muster the look of lucidity.

"Of course you can," he said, inadvertently curt. "I read your sign—Room for rent. Obviously, that's why I'm here. It is for rent?"

Chagrined, Sabella gave a uniformly terse response. "It *is* for rent, but only to the appropriate person. Perhaps that person is not you?"

Unaccustomed to anyone else assuming command, Caubi found this role reversal discomforting. Brushing the back of his hand across his forehead, he changed tack, grappling for candor.

"You're right, senhorita. I apologize. Having just woken, I didn't respond appropriately—especially to one as . . . as lovely as you. Please, accept my apology."

Face-to-face now, she responded, "Senhor, lovely has nothing to do with it."

"You're so right." An effusive bow was part of a feeble attempt to establish a penitent tone. Choreographed as a honed reflex, it was meant to establish favor with the beautiful woman standing before him.

Tempered yet remaining succinct, she said, "Yes. What can I do for you?"

Caubi wrangled an apologetic smile. "I would like to rent a room—but only if it is still available."

Scouring him from head to toe, she saw a man who had been sleeping at her doorstep while wearing fine clothing. Conflicting. Somewhat ruffled, she was made more incredulous by the gem displayed on his smooth hand.

Aware of her circumstance, she was in no position to vet this man nor reconcile his character. Being alone, with her father not expected to return for hours, she was reluctant to welcome a nameless stranger into her home, let alone show him an austere room furnished with only a bed.

Confronted with an enigma, she chose to engage him with a look of subtle levity—but at a distance, on the stoop rather than in her home. At a loss for words, exhibiting a surreptitious smile, she gently patted the man's forearm as she backed away.

"Please remain here. Let me step inside to get the paperwork. Would you like water or perhaps a glass of iced tea?"

"No, senhorita. I'll just wait here."

Nonetheless upon her return, she carried a tray with two glasses and a pitcher of water. With the papers tucked under her arm, she placed the tray on the top step, followed by a gesture for him to sit on one side while she sat on the other.

"If you wish to rent the room, it must be supplemented with a one-week deposit. If you wish to stay longer, rent would be due at the end of each month." In her mind, formality fortified their respective roles.

He smiled, stood, and stepped back for a more discerning look at the home: modestly humble and exquisitely festooned with hibiscus and brugmansia. It was a clear reflection of its host, and a modest lair in which to take root.

He sat back on the stoop. "I don't know how long I'll stay in your lovely city, senhorita." Again, he lowered his head to establish, or coerce, a more affable demeanor than his initial introduction. "It could possibly be several weeks. I'm looking for work that allows navigation on the Rio Negro. My . . . many friends from Rio have brought this type of work to my attention."

Enthusiastic, the woman raised her brow. "My father might be able to help you. He knows the river well and has land along its tributaries."

Her word selection piqued his curiosity. Wide-eyed, he quickly sat upright.

"Senhor, you're smiling. You appear surprised?"

"I'm surprised your father might know of work on the river. I look forward to meeting him."

With cocked head, the chameleon looked around, adapting to his terrain. Any tangential aspirations were, by serendipity, beginning to coalesce. But not wishing to appear overzealous, he quickly reassumed an amiable, less intimidating repose. Appearing too eager could tip his hand.

Initially dismayed by this man sleeping at her doorstep, Sabella now replaced her fleeting trepidation with the overwhelming excitement of having a paying tenant. Running her fingers hurriedly across her paperwork, she looked up with a callow smile. She found solace emanating from this potential arrangement.

"The rent is two hundred reais per week. Towels will be furnished daily. There is but one bathroom, which you will share with my father and me—but unless most necessary, only after we have departed for our work. I will understand if the inconvenience is unacceptable."

"It's fine," he answered with an unruffled flicking of the wrist, as if batting a gnat. "No inconvenience."

"Your name, senhor?" She leaned forward, craning her neck in front of him. "You do have a name?"

Although Rio was a buffering jungle away, using his given name could prove onerous. He thought quickly.

"Yes. Of course . . . Bento. Bento Cardoso."

A knee-jerk fabrication for him, the name Bento had a ring that rolled off his tongue with ease. The family name of Cardoso—the surname of a man with no tongue who once claimed to know the location of alluvial diamonds—might serve a purpose.

With a look of satisfaction, as though crossing a hurdle, he finished, "Just call me Bento."

"Mr. Bento, my name is Sabella. And yes, you can call me Sabella." Smiling and perky, she attempted to mitigate their initial rift with direct cordiality. "Mr. Bento, you now have a room. But there are formalities. The first is for your deposit, which will be returned to you if there is no damage at the time of your departure. Acceptable?"

Relieved to have a room, he reached into his shirt for a zippered purse, from which he extracted a large packet of bills. In doing so, an assortment of coins and a cellophane bag fell to the ground. Caubi quickly leaned forward, retrieving the bag and stuffing it into his shirt while leaving the coins where they fell. Unable to hide what appeared to be consternation, he simply muttered, "Too many things for such a small purse."

Sabella was surprised to see such a large cache of money in the hands of a man she had, only moments ago, found sleeping at her doorstep. It would be presumptuous to place him in a specific social class, especially having met him so recently. The contents of the cellophane bag didn't go unnoticed, either.

But because he was a paying guest, she chose to brush off these conscious thoughts. Rather, she chose to assume he was simply an eccentric of some means.

"Mr. Bento, my father and I are grateful that you will be renting a room," she said, wishing to engage her new tenant with a sense of belonging. Then she lowered her voice and confided, "For some, well . . . these are difficult times."

Following a muted "I see," he collected his duffel and was escorted to his room. He looked forward to meeting her father. Sleep came easily once again as he lay down for a nap.

Relieved to have found an additional source of income, Sabella sat alone in her kitchen. It was at least an initial step out of their dilemma. Folding the money, she placed it in a shoebox, wedging it behind the pipes beneath the sink.

She was excited to share the news.

Chapter Ten

Discerning people can see what happens before their
very eyes. Constrained people, only when courageous,
may recognize it for what it really is.

THE BMW AIRHEAD HAD A DRONE that always caught her attention. Never late, it was music to her ears. Sabella could set her watch to the minute as João parked the motorcycle in front of her home.

Soon after meeting at the university, João and Sabella started seeing each other exclusively. They shared more than the intellectual harvest of academics. Because of that which was inherent, some men took perverse, if not preconceived sordid, liberties, going so far as to decry her as the femme fatale of Manaus. This knowledge kept João vigilant while it kept Sabella circumspect, yet comforted and secure.

Running on quiet tiptoes to the door, Sabella cautiously opened the screen and slipped outside. First, she placed fingers to pursed lips, but then she jumped in place and feigned clapping, forgoing the sound.

Caught unawares by her excitement, João was unable to restrain a puzzled smile. He placed accepting hands on her waist, lifted her from the porch, and twirled her above the stoop.

With knees bent, she kicked up her heels and let out a gasp. "We have a tenant!" she whispered. "Finally, we have a tenant who has already given a down payment."

"What's the quiet for?" burst João in a louder volume than he intended.

Shaking her head, she quickly placed a finger to his lips. "He's sleeping. I don't want to wake him."

Always virile, João threw her over his shoulder and danced down the stairs. After turning a few circles, he placed her on the cobbled walkway for a tiptoe dance.

"We gotta go to town and celebrate," he whispered this time.

Wide-eyed and childlike, Sabella gripped her cheeks. "Oh, but we can't leave. Not now—not until Papai returns. He doesn't know we're landlords. He might mistake our new tenant for an intruder and throw him into the street."

With an impish grin, she circled João like a pugilist in the ring, teasing with finger pokes into his stomach.

"Hello," came a low-pitched interjection from behind the screen door.

Immediately stiffened, the startled couple turned to see a shadow with no discernable features.

"Senhor Cardoso," Sabella said awkwardly, frozen in place. "We're sorry for waking you." She extended her palms toward João as an apologetic introduction. "This is João, my betrothed. João, this is Mr. Bento Cardoso, our new tenant."

Opening the screen with his foot, Caubi stepped onto the porch. He appeared unusually secure, considering he had entered this home for the first time only a short while ago. His movements, slow and mechanical, expressed familiarity—almost an implied ownership.

"*Olá,* Senhor Cardoso," was João's tempered greeting.

He placed a protective arm around Sabella's shoulder. He immediately began sizing up the man who stood tall before him, arms across his chest, wearing both a surreptitious smile and a slouched leather fedora. It was an unusual display for one just awakened from a sound sleep.

"Mr. Cardoso, João attends the local university, as do I, and he works as a part-time stevedore with my father," Sabella said. "They both know the Rio Negro. He too may be able to help you find work."

With that, Caubi jumped from the stoop, congenial once more "Yes. Yes, yes, yes. I'd like that," he said, conspicuously affable.

Doing his best to quell a look of perplexity, João wondered what to think of this man's demeanor. Slightly obtrusive, it evoked a sense of both guarded and competitive unease. Both men, marginally animated, said little as they looked at each other. Turf was being set. João slowly circled the stranger, finding him both bizarre and unpleasant.

As an inadvertently estranged third party, Sabella found herself glancing back and forth from João to her new tenant. She flitted as a referee, sidestepping along the walkway while straddling a row of potted desert rose.

If João wished to yield the man some slack, he would acknowledge that most people might perform similarly in a new or uncomfortable setting. On this occasion, however, there would be no slack. Instead, João questioned this man's intentions. Was he after Sabella—or something else?

Stepping forward with confidence, the recently christened Bento Cardoso extended his arm for a handshake. Willfully positioned as a pawn, he had completed the opening move of a chess match.

"Could we discuss what possibilities might exist? Say, over a drink? It is clear we all have reason to celebrate." He cocked his head to one side. "After all, I am your new client, a position I believe satisfies each of us?"

João could not help but sense that this man—of whom he knew nothing—was taking command. His pompous eloquence was mystifying, especially for one looking for work. The pawns were being set. A bind was being established. The match was underway.

Still, feeling obligated to acquiesce, João accepted the offer. His purposeful response was an attempt to at least make this encounter brief.

"Let's go to Guillermo's Bistro, then . . . it's close." Turning, he looked at an empty street. "We can either walk three kilometers or ride all three on my motorcycle." This wasn't an arrangement to João's liking, but, all considered, it was the only option.

"Riding three isn't unusual," Sabella interjected. "Even Papai rides with us."

Caubi's quick and unassuming response left no room for debate. "Three it is."

Sabella nodded, then stepped quickly onto the stoop. "I must leave Papai a note. He'll be worried if we're not here."

Clearly, he was pivotal in her mind—an advantageous revelation for the new guest.

Sabella ran inside to leave her papai a note and was back out on the stoop in a flash, ready to go. João was already on the motorcycle. She took her place behind him, wrapping her arms around his waist. Caubi took the back, all too eager to place his palms high and secure on Sabella's sides.

To João's consternation, Sabella didn't seem compromised by the configuration. She perceived her new tenant's grasp to be a matter of safety and not an affront to her dignity.

As they reached the bistro, Caubi led the way by jumping off the motorcycle, quickly assuming the role of maître d' by opening the door with an arm extended.

Squeezing past Sabella, João tucked his chin and, beneath his breath, mumbled, "*Quem diabos é esse cara?*"— Who the hell is this guy?

Caubi raised his arm and snapped his fingers, summoning the man standing behind the counter.

Startled, Guillermo jumped to attention, running to the door only to be greeted by João and Sabella. Both rolled their eyes as a stealthy, nonverbal apology to their longtime friend—the bistro's owner, maître d', and host. Following a quick introduction, he seated them in a corner booth. Sabella and João stared at each other as Guillermo walked away, throwing both hands in the air.

But almost instantly, Caubi once again summoned their host. "Cachaça. Very strong." This request was inconsistent not only with the time of day but also his newly acquired rank of boarder.

João, shaking his head in bewilderment, ordered a flavored tea. Sabella, still enamored with having a new patron—though not necessarily *by* the new patron—ordered a Campari with orange juice. A little tart but nevertheless a friend to her palate. She winked at João, whose questioning smile was punctuated with a shrug.

Once the drinks arrived, the conversation slipped into inquiries that set Sabella and João on edge. The man they knew as Bento was unusually curious not only about the river but its tributaries.

"Has anyone ever exploited them for profit?" he asked.

His word selection couldn't have been more repulsive.

Her hackles raised, Sabella leaned forward, firmly pressing both of her index fingers on the table. "The only people who see 'profits' from those waters are the loggers who rape our land and the fortune hunters who pilfer antiquities from our native people," she said. It was a fluid diatribe, delivered with punctate indignation, from a woman who carried a resolute love for the river and the land.

João took hold of her hand as a calming gesture and nodded his approval. Their shared passions extended beyond the amorous. To prove their solidarity, he stood, placing both knuckled hands on the table. "Just what did you have in mind, Mr. Cardoso?"

Caubi realized he had struck a chord. Nevertheless, he remained undeterred as he alternated between briefly glimpsing at Sabella and directly staring at João.

"I mean no harm. Your world, your forest, is lush and beautiful. But it only stands to reason there must be treasures for those willing to work. In fact, I have it on good authority that one could possibly find gems in the waters near your lovely city."

It was clear to João that their new acquaintance had a flair for words that served little purpose, save his own. Who was this "authority" the man spoke of? For his part, João had always understood that alluvial diamonds were rare on the Rio Negro.

Clutching hands beneath the table, Sabella and João now shared a similar opinion: there was more to this man than they knew.

Sabella indelicately placed her glass on the table. "It's time to leave," she said shortly. "Papai will be home soon."

Indeed, when they arrived, Sabella's father was standing on the porch, waving his arms, holding the note in his hand. Exceedingly enthusiastic, he embraced his daughter, then shook João's hand as if it were a pump handle. Wide-eyed and with an expansive smile, Abilio looked fawningly at his new tenant.

Caubi stepped forward without enticement and with welcoming outstretched arms. "Greetings. I'm so very pleased to meet you," he said. "Your beautiful daughter has told me wonderful things about you."

Oblivious, Abilio was as fodder, putty in Caubi's hands.

Chapter Eleven

Steeped in need and vulnerable when chained to
naivete—thus defined the obsequious father of Sabella
the Redeemer. Hearing only what one wishes to hear
comes easy. Everyone does it. Papai's Good Shepherd
had arrived.

THOROUGHLY APPRISED OF THEIR NEW TENANT—including his peculiarities—Abilio was relieved. Having slept well, he rose early, vibrant, and excited. With hope's door opened, he enthusiastically paced quietly in front of his new friend's room. Finally, the door opened.

"Senhor Bento. Good morning, my new friend. You are an early riser. That is good." Bobbing his head, Abilio clasped his hands at his chest and circled his tenant. The scene was set. "My daughter has informed me of your wishes. You are excited to get on with your first day of explorations, yes?"

The man known as Bento could have been clad in tights and a tutu, yet Abilio still would have seen only that which he wanted to see: a man with obvious wealth retrieving *dinheiro* from his river.

From the other side, Caubi knew exactly what he was seeing: a pull toy to which he, Caubi, held the string.

With short, quick steps, Abilio waddled to the man, who with no effort had become bigger than life. In the next moment, he stepped back with a subservient, wide-eyed expression and approved every detail of his tenant from head to toe. A blind man could have done the same.

"Oh, Senhor Bento. I must protect you. We will be forest walking. You must dress more properly."

With a mesmerized gaze fixed on his tenant, Abilio hurriedly backed up toward a corner closet. Retrieving a duffel, he emptied its contents onto the floor. Rubber boots, gloves, a long-sleeved shirt, and leather leggings spilled out.

Returning to his tenant's side, Abilio rubbed his hands along the man's arm as if caressing an icon. "I am so sorry," he said apologetically, "but you must wear a long-sleeved shirt and gloves. There are many sharp branches and grasses that will cut your hands and arms. There are also insects and spiders." Leaning forward at the waist, slowly shaking his head, he continued, "That would not be good."

With Abilio as low-hanging fruit on a pliable limb, Caubi reached out and grasped the older man by the shoulders. "*Obrigado.* You can be my teacher. I'll follow you to the wharf or wherever you would like me to be."

Once again, his words fell on deaf ears. Abilio didn't hear, see, or witness the man before him. He saw hope. Taking his tenant by the hand, he said, "Please follow me."

Only, Abilio didn't realize it was Caubi who was leading.

As they rode the morning trolley to the river, Abilio sat with his knees together and hands clasped in his lap. His eyes were fixed on his new tenant.

Trolley passengers, mostly dockworkers, extended their morning greetings to Abilio. He, in turn, introduced them not to "Senhor Cardoso," but to "Bento, my new friend." By the time they arrived at the pier, Caubi was not only looked upon with favor—he belonged.

As if leading a child, Abilio continued to hold his friend Bento's hand, bringing him to a handcrafted wooden skiff moored at the end of a dilapidated pier.

Abilio enthusiastically rubbed his hands together before helping his new friend into the skiff. "Now we begin."

They slowly motored the Rio Negro in Abilio's boat. The journey, although slow, was not arduous. Quite the contrary, as expectations were high for both.

En route, Abilio pointed to an embankment on the far side of the river. Small white crosses stippled the hillside. "My lovely wife, Sabella's mother. That is her resting place," he said quietly. "I always say a prayer over her when traveling to the land. May I?"

"Of course, my dear friend. Anything you wish," Caubi expressed with an air of reverence.

After maneuvering the skiff to the shore, Abilio scrambled up the sandy hill on all fours, repeatedly looking back as if seeking his tenant's approval. Kneeling at a cross adorned by a flowered wreath, Abilio looked down the hill once again, sharing his piety as he crossed himself.

Shielding his impatience, Caubi sat twiddling his thumbs behind the gunwales of the skiff. Wishing to appear a part of Abilio's theatrics, he quickly raised his hands, holding them together as if joining the moment of prayer.

When Abilio returned to the skiff, it was apparent he had been crying.

Caubi's only thought: *Beautifully pathetic.*

Although long and hot, the day was abundantly rewarding. The river's tributaries were as endless fingers, their sources reaching far into terra firma. Abilio and Caubi traveled for hours, passing barges filled with sediment obtained from the river's bottom.

Abilio's land was concealed deep along the periphery of the water's web, invisibly etched inland along minor rivulets. Caubi knew there was no foreseeable way to pursue a productive search of the river bottom here. It was simply too expansive. There would be no retrieval of alluvial diamonds—despite what Caubi would lead Abilio to believe.

Rather, Caubi found this secluded land to be especially satisfying for a more lucrative alternative. His plan was already framed with a literally animate conduit at the ready—Captain Helmut Richter.

Just then, serendipity approached in the form of a menacing bow wave that caused Abilio to veer sharply to the side of the river. The source of the wave was a tug towing a flat-bottomed barge fully loaded with fresh-cut lumber. It was exiting a channel running along Abilio's land.

Abilio gave a furtive nod toward the helmsman. Tucking his chin while wearing an undeniable grimace, he exuded transgression.

This silent admission of guilt didn't go unnoticed by Caubi. As a child, he had witnessed this same expression in unseasoned men and boys darting ashamedly from his mother's room.

Caubi knew this tug and barge represented an operation that generally should have been conducted beneath a new moon. To the desperate souls as well as to the unabashedly evil at heart, removing trees—the sinew of that which made up the essence of the rain forest—was fraught with risk and consequence.

Abilio, indelibly chafed and weakened, could not conceal his misdeed. His veritable soul was visibly crushed, with Caubi as the silent satanical witness.

Yet his questions were insidious and seemingly indifferent. "Who was that man, Abilio? Why was he pulling the lumber?"

Stumbling, Abilio's response again telegraphed remorse, even as he attempted to deflect blame. "Whoever did this, it's only . . . only from one tree. It won't be missed. It has no great value. What they're doing isn't so bad. It will help feed a good family and ease the hardship they may have encountered. The officials will let it pass. It is only one tree."

He was exposed.

Caubi's relationship with Abilio strategically realigned. As a pigeon, Abilio's value increased.

Twiddling his thumbs for a new reason, Caubi leaned into the bow and crossed his ankles over the starboard gunwale. Nonchalant and cunning, his retort was simple: "Abilio, I'm anxious to see the land of which you're so proud. Might it be good for crops?"

Immersed in guilt, the older man's gaze was fixed on the motor. "No, Mr. Bento. The forest must not be destroyed. We protect the forest. Our trees make the air we breathe."

Caubi smiled condescendingly as he listened to words wrapped in a lie. Increasingly comforted, he folded his hands behind his head, shifted slightly, and crossed his ankles over the portside rail. Turning his head, he panned across the clouds so as not to overplay his hand.

"Abilio, can we do some of what you call forest walking? Forest walking . . . on *your* land?"

The emphasis on "your" implied ownership and respect. As Caubi anticipated, the word resurrected a submissive smile from Abilio. Restoring pride has purpose.

"I wish to see your land," Caubi continued. "Land which is distant, quiet, and private. Land where one can be free. Land where no one goes. Land where there is peace. Do you understand?"

His words caressed, flowed. Abilio, the subservient fiddle, was played.

Clinging between recompense and despair, Abilio breathed a sigh of relief. Like a thirsty basin, he was now being filled with hope.

"Of course, my friend." Abilio stood enthusiastically. Steadying himself at the stern while holding the handle of the motor, he pointed to the river's edge. "We must follow these channels. Because the river changes with the seasons, I have marked the way with tassels in the trees. They are not visible unless you search for them." Assuming authority once again, he continued. "In one kilometer, we will begin forest walking. It isn't difficult. The canopy is dense and gives shade to the forest floor. There is very little undergrowth. I know these things."

With a smile, Caubi nodded.

Both were pleased.

The walk proved rewarding. Abilio's land extended nearly two kilometers away from the Rio Negro. Allowing Abilio to retain his secret, Caubi knew there would be no more need for solitary tugs and barges towing singular trees. Saving face and achieving objectives—a win-win for both.

"We can return on another day to begin sifting the river bottom for more of the treasure I wear on my finger," Caubi said, waving his hand in Abilio's face—a magician's sleight.

Selectively, Abilio both saw and heard.

They returned home well after dark; Sabella and João had anxiously awaited their arrival. They and the man known as Bento listened as Abilio described the day in detail. He left out the chance meeting with the tug towing lumber.

"And Mr. Bento shared our loss by visiting your mother's grave."

Sabella and João carefully glanced at each other. As best they could, they hid their head shakes and cringes.

But once again, this secret communication did not go unnoticed by Caubi. Knowing he had fences to mend, he remained silent, letting his newly appointed pawn pave what he perceived would be a more amicable path for the ensuing days. He knew that Abilio's happiness, although misdirected, would eventually allay their initial fears.

Softly spoken, with a ploy of reverence, Caubi finally spoke. Smartly, he addressed Sabella. "Your most kind father has offered to direct me to those who can assist in my exploration tomorrow. I am most grateful. It has been a long and trying day, and I wouldn't have managed without your capable father." He bowed his head. "I believe it would be best if I were to retire for the evening."

Practically bursting with pride, Abilio danced to this man's lead, suggesting he would do the same.

Not knowing how to direct the conversation, Sabella finally gave her father an assuring hug and kissed him on the cheek. "João and I are pleased to see you so happy, Papai," she said. Looking at João, she felt the evening's finale had been reached. "We should all rest."

That night, Caubi reconfigured his plan. While Abilio was currently a fragile but invaluable widget, he would eventually become an obstruction standing between Caubi and loftier goals.

The following day, Abilio summoned dockworkers who would supply the tools his friend Bento needed.

Meanwhile, Caubi walked to a more distant pier. Captain Richter stood erect on the bridge, overseeing his workers as they loaded his vessel with motorcycles and undisclosed sundries for transport to Trinidad, the ABC islands, and ports beyond. With anticipation, he watched Caubi board his vessel.

Looking piercingly into Caubi's eyes, Richter listened as Caubi methodically outlined his plan. When the young man finished, the captain patted him on both shoulders and nodded with quick approval. The men shook hands.

Caubi sauntered down the gangplank, pumping his fists. With a thumbs-up, he turned for another look at Richter. Smiling, Caubi extended his chin and placed the fingers of both hands to his lips before casting his arms out wide. He followed that with an exuberant wallah salute toward the bridge.

Chapter Twelve

For those innately ensconced or fixed by circumstance,
time, and place—a change in the ambient milieu, be it
by complexion or temperature, may prove an arduous
reckoning.

NOAH WAS A MAN CONSUMED, on a singular mission. Now distorted and reconfigured as an automaton, he flew from Boston to Brazil and made his way through São Paulo's Guarulhos International Airport to board a domestic flight to Manaus.

Out of his element, he was imperiled by uncertainty and driven by unyielding anger. Oblivious to what he had once been, he remained blindly unaware of what he had become. Clenched teeth, tight fists, and a condescending sneer defined the man.

In this godforsaken place, he saw dark faces glaring at him with disdain. In reality, he was seeing a reflection of himself, as if peering into a looking glass. His expression was critical, searching, as he dissected his surroundings. He carried with him the calamitous memory of angry faces as seen through a lattice of bougainvillea.

Upon takeoff, he gazed through his window, watching as the smog-eclipsed city of São Paulo was replaced by a perpetual carpet of green.

Consumed, Noah failed to recognize that beneath the verdant canopy, there existed real people. Some strong, some weak, and a waning few holding secrets of the ages. Evil stood alone.

He also failed to realize there existed an expansive epitaph etched by travail and injustice. Myopic by preconception, he knew nothing of the greed that inundated Brazil from all directions—not the history of the rubber barons from America and Europe, nor the diaspora of slaves from Africa.

Waging a philosophical war within himself, he closed his eyes, searching for refuge from his unremitting turmoil. He mused over that which all beings share—want.

He wanted Jessie. That wouldn't happen. She was at peace. For the unreconciled few, death might be accepted as a means for lasting peace. He wondered whether we were as lemmings, tumbling endlessly without recourse, or whether there was a preordained end.

As a precocious child, he had had time to conjure myriad distracted thoughts such as these. These meanderings of an untainted youth brought comfort. Solace could be found between the covers of a book, but mostly it came from within.

However, that *within* no longer existed for Noah. Now there would be a reckoning. He wanted revenge. Might that bring fulfillment?

Or might it lead to perpetual atonement?

Startled by a sudden downdraft, Noah stiffened. "What the—" he blurted.

"Buddy, you okay?" came from the middle seat.

Stunned, wide-eyed, and with his mouth agape, Noah momentarily appeared to struggle with where he was. Looking side to side, raising his brow, he took a deep breath. "Ah, yeah. Sorry. I guess I was sleeping . . . or daydreaming."

Collecting himself, Noah turned to realize he was seated next to a white man. Most of the other passengers were brown, black, or something in between. Dressed in khaki, the man wore a safari hat, its brim turned up on the side.

With a look of inquiring perplexity, Noah pointed. "Your hat—do a lot of people wear hats like that? I mean, turned up on the side?"

The man tweaked his mouth in an ingratiating smile. "Mostly the fancy Dans. Me, I just like it." He paused. "Strange question. Why ya askin'?"

"Just curious. Are you Brazilian?"

With a smile, not wishing to seem condescending, the man suppressed a chuckle with a question of his own. "What's a Brazilian look like?" He smiled and looked down, as if to scrutinize his own torso. "Do I look Brazilian? No, sir. I'm an American, but I live in Brazil. Manaus to be exact. 'Bout thirty years now."

"Why'd you ever want to live there? I mean, in another country?"

The man raised one side of his upper lip, furrowed his brow, and nodded, suggesting approval of Noah's quizzical nature.

"So ya wanna know why I'm here, do ya? I'll tell ya. I'm from Rocky Knob, Tennessee. Was in a rat race. Never knowin' where my next check was comin' from. Heard there was money to be made, so I came here, worked the mines up in the northeast. More clean iron than ya ever saw. Brazil is rich. Iron country. Cutthroat. Life means nothin'—least to some of 'em. If you think life is screwed up in the States, you ain't seen nothin'."

Noah wished he had never asked.

"More Indians killed here than in the Wild West," his seatmate continued. "Natives got screwed. Everyone screwed 'em. Poor little devils. Anyway, got outta iron country and wound up in Manaus. Was a rich place once. Rubber then. Now it's duty-free crap—electronics, motorcycles. No roads. Can't even drive outta the place. Just ships and planes . . . in and out. Like living on an island in the middle of nowhere."

Noah nodded, wanting out but nevertheless being drawn in. "So you . . . don't like it here."

Elevating one eyebrow and turning his head slowly toward Noah, the man lowered his chin. "Nah. I like it here. There's a lot to learn. Gotta know the people, what they went through. Not understanding it gets ya in trouble. I learnt it . . . kinda the hard way."

Not interested in the sermon that threatened to follow, Noah sought to detour the subject. "Why'd you stay in Manaus?"

The man's smile returned. He leaned back in his seat, placing folded hands over his belly while focusing on the overhead bin.

"I'll tell ya. Did what other people did: bought me a woman. I got me a job selling bibelots, set up shop, and bought me a woman."

"What! You bought a woman?" Jutting his chin, Noah turned to face the man directly. "I mean, you actually . . . *bought* a person. An actual *person*?"

With a quick jerk of his head and a reciprocating, protruding chin, Noah was now nose to nose with the man.

"You damn right I did," he countered. "And she's 'ppreciative. I fed 'er, housed 'er, and clothed 'er. She's good to me, and I'm good to her. She's like most of her kind—half this and half that and half everything else."

Shaking an instructional finger, the man continued. "Let me tell ya. Her people go way back. Survived in the bush. When the early foreigners came—ya know, to bring 'em religion—the bush people were treated like animals. Rumor has it, they were put in pens. Some even say they were gaffed like pigs—pulled out of the pens, gutted, then roasted and eaten. Yep," he said to Noah's incredulous look. "Why? 'Cuz the foreigners were starvin' to death in the green hell, and some preacher declared the bush people not human."

Noah grimaced, stared, and pumped both index fingers directly toward the stranger's chest—all the while grappling for words.

The man on the other end of this reaction didn't know whether Noah was admonishing him because he appeared to have a sordid nuptial arrangement or because he had simply shared his insight on the squalor of the wretched aborigines below.

"Hold on, buddy. My wife was snatched from the bush as a babe," the man said. "Rules say she can't go back. Not legal. Letting her people live like they did for a thousand years. She grew up takin' care of kids and cleaning house for some missionary schoolteacher. My wife was totin' his kids and lookin' for a buggy when I found her. She had a look. Uncanny. Smart. So I asked her to work for me. Minister said no at first. I said I'd take her off his hands for a box of old Bibles. So stuck in his religion, he took me up on my offer. I bought her for twenty bucks and a box of worn-out Gideons. So much for religion."

Bobbing his head and slowly rubbing his chin, the man now appeared candidly embarrassed. "On second thought, maybe *she* found *me*. Now I think I'm working for her!"

Noah was now sitting well over the edge of his seat, slowly turning his head side to side. "Amazing." Now he was willfully drawn into the fold. "You have kids? A family?"

"No. No kids. She had some disease. Brazil has 'em— weird diseases. Ya know, the real killers were imports, from Europe. If it didn't kill the bush people, it made some of 'em sterile. Good thing for me, though. I have a tough time with kids, especially poor Brazil kids. Some of 'em gotta be beggars and thieves, just to live." Now in command, he assumed an advisory demeanor. "You gotta lot to learn, kid.

Learn it. Oh"—he leaned back and extended his hand—"name's Jack. Folks here call me Amazon Jack."

Flustered by the rapid transition, Noah assumed cordiality, though with a hint of reluctance. He slowly accepted the handshake. "Okay, Mr. . . . Jack. I'm Noah. Ah, just Noah."

"Well, just Noah, now ya know about me." With a cursory head-to-toe inspection, he said, "You're a scrawny-looking paleface. What brings ya to the green hell?"

"What do you mean, 'green hell'?"

Jack shook his head. "To the point: Why ya here?"

As an attempt to literally change the direction this conversation was headed, Noah turned away to face the window. "Just looking."

Jack cupped his ear and leaned forward. "Speak up. Just what—or who—is it you're looking for?"

With an abrupt turn, Noah looked directly at Jack. "I . . . I'm not sure."

An inquisitive Amazon Jack shook his head—pleasant, almost fatherly.

"Fella, there's about a couple million people in Manaus. It's gonna be special hard if you don't know what yer lookin' for."

Noah conveyed an accepting yet evasive nod. "I'll know him—or them—when I see 'em. Maybe. There's something about an opera house."

"Well, I hope ya know what yer doin'. This is one tough place. Get outta line being a new whitey, and you're screwed. Screwed good. The States—a piece of cake. Here—just plain screwed."

Jack leaned back, putting his head on the rest. Diluting himself with vodka, he hung his hat over his knee and covered his head and face with a towel. Pacified by the drone of the engines, he went to sleep. For the ensuing two hours, nothing more was said.

Noah sat with a disjointed potpourri of thoughts—a trinket shop, a broad-brimmed safari hat, a woman bought for a box of Bibles. *What in the hell kind of a place is this?* Returning to the window, he remained lost in the wonderment of the never-ending blanket of green.

As though triggered by a timer, Amazon Jack stirred, removed the towel, and replaced his hat, appearing wide awake just before the plane began its descent.

"Get any sleep, kid?"

"No. Just thinking." With an ineffectual attempt to suppress naivete, he gestured to the window. "Look—I see it. See? Down there. The Amazon River."

Accompanied by a guttural chuckle, Jack's smile returned. He shook his head. "Nah, that's not it. That's just a trickle dumpin' into the big one."

Confused, Noah said, "I haven't seen much water for several hours."

"That's 'cuz it's covered. Thousands of rivers all covered by the green hell. If you're here for any time, you'll learn what I mean. Depending on our approach comin' in, you'll see the black one or the brown one. They hook up just outside of Manaus. We're not there yet. Another thirty minutes. But you ain't seen nothin' till you've seen the big one."

With lips pursed and cheeks puffed, Jack exercised another slow up-and-down gaze at Noah. He didn't mince words. "You're too damn scrawny. You'll melt in no time. Looks like ya got a wrench in your gut. Let it out. Ease up. Either that or harden your will. Live here long enough, you'll become a saint."

Noah couldn't hide a look of surprise. Years previous, he'd heard a similar expression after a long night in the operating room. One of his mentors had simply said, "If travail hardens the will, neurosurgery leads to sainthood." The statement had resonated then. And hearing it now—from this transplant from nowhere—made Noah wonder and look twice at the man next to him.

Maybe this bumpkin has more going for him than I thought, he mused.

"Well, skinny, look at 'er," Jack said, pointing out the window. "The big one. They write entire books about 'er. Kid, she gets even bigger as she moves east."

With his forehead pressed against the portside window, Noah craned his neck to look down. There she was—the Amazon—undulating like a giant serpent. Brown and black, she carved her way through a desolate never-ending carpet of green.

A drawn-out, astonished "Holy jeez" was all he could muster.

"Yeah, kid, she grabs me that way too. Depending on her mood, you can love 'er or hate 'er . . . but never at the same time. If you're here long enough, you might find that out."

Raising his brow while fabricating a gaping yawn, Noah cleared his ears as the plane made its descent. Looking at

Jack, he said, "I guess this is where I start . . . ?" It was delivered as a quasi question.

Without a Jetway, the passengers disembarked directly onto the hot concrete of the tarmac. The air was thick, with no escape from the suffocating heat.

Noah's initial introduction to Manaus—caustic. It was like stepping onto a frying pan inside a blast furnace.

Bustling from the plane, the other passengers took it in stride as everyone filed into a narrow room with gray stucco walls and louvered windows. Guarded and unsettled, Noah Garrett was alone in a room filled with foreigners. Even when encountering them in their own homeland, he immediately labeled them as foreigners.

"They're gonna sift through your bags, fella," he heard a voice say behind him.

Turning, he saw Amazon Jack with a dripping brow and shirt already made transparent from sweat. Now Noah didn't feel quite so alone. There was something refreshing about the man. Rather funny looking, with a Durante nose, he was nevertheless comfortable in his own skin.

An admirable trait, Noah thought. *Like my father, but easier.*

Amazon Jack ran both hands down his dripping torso. "You never really get used to it. The heat, I mean. But look all around ya. Not a lick of sweat on the locals—just us. I've been here for the better part of thirty years and look at me—still bleedin' this ooze." Jack rolled his eyes and laughed. "Course, most of these drippings is due to that cheap vodka they poured down my neck on the plane." He gave Noah a sheepish grin. "Stay away from the booze, kid."

Without a word, Noah grimaced and tugged at his shirt, which was indeed clinging with sweat. He wiped his brow, though new beads formed before he could even lower his hand.

Ahead, the sea of passengers began to move. With his carry-on held snugly and defensively under his arm, Noah followed the others to the baggage claim, where his luggage was searched to the last item.

While packing, he had considered bringing a knife or even a gun. He was glad he hadn't. It had been a convoluted idea conjured under duress. It would not have served him well. Such ideas seldom do.

As he reassembled his carry-on, Noah noticed a business card left for him on the table. "Amazon Jack of All Trades," it read. "I buy, sell, barter, and trade curios, bric-a-brac, and the ultimate collectable." On the back of the card, he had scribbled, "Tour guide and translation information: English and Portuguese." It also said, "Good luck, whitey."

But Jack was nowhere to be seen.

Bizarre how a person can find comfort with a stranger when stuck in God knows where.

Outside, Noah sprinted along the curb, dragging his bags behind him. He waved his arm while whistling and yelling "Cabby!" It made him the consummate outsider, sticking out like a sore thumb.

"Looking for a ride, skinny?"

It was Jack, now a passenger in a rusted '50-something VW bus. He was a welcome sight as the van pulled to the curb.

"Ah, Mr. Jack," Noah said, relieved.

With his arms crossed and broad shoulders leaning out the window, Jack appeared to be alone in the vehicle. Standing on his toes, Noah strained to see the driver, who remained out of sight.

"Where ya stayin'?" Jack asked.

"The Santos. The Hotel Santos."

"Good. Not far from our place. Close to the market. Don't just stand there. Get in."

Noah wedged himself into the back seat, which was cluttered with boxes and statuary. Even now, he saw nothing but what appeared to be an empty driver's seat.

Jack turned and threw his arm over the seat. "It's Noah, right?" With an expression synonymous with pride, Jack then extended his right hand toward the driver's seat. "Noah, this is my wife, Flora. Told you 'bout her."

As if ascending from nowhere, a woman put her knee on the front seat to boost herself as she strained her neck to peer over her headrest. She was all teeth with an exuberant, welcoming smile.

"Jack said you needed a ride. He always picks up strangers." Reaching across the seat, she patted Jack on the shoulder. "He's a good man. He's good that way."

This diminutive woman with copper skin and shiny black hair looked at him with unrestrained acceptance. She nodded, her smile growing larger.

Unwittingly, Noah did reveal tarnish, yet this unassuming woman exuded such a sense of ease and approval that it caused his demeanor to momentarily transform into a look of pleasantry.

"Okay, the Santos it is," Jack announced, and Flora started them on their way. "Not the greatest hotel, but not too bad. By the looks of ya, the roaches are in better shape than you."

"What do you mean, 'roaches'?"

"Lot of crawly critters around the market, you know—with the fish and all. Some mangy people too."

"Is it okay, though? I mean, safe?"

"Keep your nose clean, and it'll be safe enough. But why ya stayin' there?"

"It was the only place with a room not far from the opera house," Noah expressed with an unsettled look.

"There ya go again—the opera house. Skinny, you look and talk sort of sophisticated, but I never took you for an opera nut."

"I'm not. But that's where I have to be. I mean . . . where I have to start."

Jack looked Noah over from head to toe. "Skinny, what in hell are ya here for? I don't like to butt into people's lives, but there's something rippin' at ya. You in trouble? Are ya lookin'. . . or runnin'?"

"I—I'm not running. I'm looking. And my name is Noah. Noah Garrett. Not 'skinny.' I'm Noah Garrett."

"Okay, Noah Garrett. What in hell ya lookin' for?"

With an aggravated swallow, Noah shook his head. "Someone. Just someone."

Little more was said; the ride was brief. Soon enough, Flora pulled to the curb.

"This, Mr. Noah Garrett, is it." Sliding down in his seat, Jack pointed out his window. "Your hotel. The Santos.

But before you get too settled, you might want to reconsider—your room, I mean. Manaus may be in the middle of nowhere, but we do have other hotels. More, well, American-like."

"No, this'll be okay. Close to the opera house. Like I said—a place to start."

Squeezing from the restrictive confines of the van, Noah thanked Flora and Jack for the ride.

"If you need anything—bibelots or directions, anything—you have my card. Just come on by." Jack looked at the diminutive mite in the front seat with noticeable affection. "If I'm not there, Flo knows where to find me. She knows this city like the palm of her hand."

Noah maneuvered his bags from the van and thanked his escorts once again. As they drove off, he stood on the cobbled walk and looked up at the structure he would, with reluctance, call home.

Stepping through a sun-blistered door led Noah immediately into a foyer that was little more than a cubicle. Rigorously simple, it was furnished with one high-backed rattan chair and a fashionable burgundy settee. Behind an ornate wooden counter sat a man with his back to the door. Oblivious to Noah's presence, he appeared glued to a television attached precariously to the wall.

Trying not to be inappropriately intrusive yet wanting to capture the man's attention, Noah simply cleared his throat and whispered, "Sir?"

Although initially startled, the man turned, robotically slow. His eyes were swollen, consistent with having been aroused from a deep sleep. He looked old, his face resembling leather. To Noah's surprise, he also looked friendly.

"*Senhor, o que posso fazer por você?*"

"Sorry. I—I don't speak, uh, Portuguese. That's Portuguese?"

The man nodded, his smile widening. "Oh, yes, sir, it is Portuguese. But I speak English very good. You're the *americano*? I have been expecting you."

"I am. I've reserved a room. The name is Garrett. Noah Garrett."

Noah looked around the foyer. In addition to the chair and settee, there was one cockeyed picture of a full-bearded, uniformed man wearing a high-collared jacket adorned with medals. The picture, unfamiliar to him, just added to the oddity of the room.

At first, Noah assumed the walls had been antiqued to mimic an aged appearance. With scrutiny, however, he realized this was no fabricated effect. The walls were the real thing: old, cracked, and stained from years of simply existing. The motif and the old man bore a striking similarity.

The room also held a muted odor, keeping with its vintage decor. Behind the desk were pigeonholes for occupants' mail. All were noticeably empty.

Noah was gripped with the incalculable feeling of being alone. Until Jessie, being alone had been acceptable, his way of life. But now this was different, foreign. He was no longer on familiar turf.

"My name is José." Panning his gaze across the room, the man continued with a slow introductory wave of an extended arm. "I am the manager of this fine hotel. And you, sir, are *my* first americano guest."

How José could live there or even equate it to a fine hotel was difficult for Noah to fathom. Nevertheless, the man seemed both sincere and accommodating.

He handed Noah a pencil, which he presented with both hands as a formal gesture. "Here, Senhor Garrett— you sign the registration book on the desk. Then I'll escort you to your room!" His excited, anticipatory expression and the tenor of his voice implied a surprise was coming.

José scooped up Noah's bags and eagerly led the way. As they climbed along a creaking staircase, the hotel aroused Noah's curiosity. At the far end of an otherwise-darkened corridor, a single light was strategically positioned over an arcane Spanish giltwood mirror. Slightly tilted, the glass was wavy, and the reflected images were eerily distorted, making it nonfunctional and bizarre in Noah's eyes. Nothing made any sense in this upside-down part of the world.

Hastening his steps, José displayed an air of escalating excitement. At the end of the corridor, he abruptly stopped, assumed an erect military posture, and dropped Noah's bags. With palms up, he extended both arms.

"This, Senhor Garrett, will be your room. It is lovely, and it is quiet. As an americano, you will find it especially appropriate." He opened the door, extended one arm, and dipped his chin, exuding both finesse and decorum. "Do enter."

The room, unlike the corridor, radiated warmth. The neoclassical carpet was both elegant and serene, with soft saffron-lavender tones set off by pale greens and blues. An Indo-Portuguese bed sat angled in the corner with side tables and chairs to match. Noah found the room enticing, tasteful, classic, and clean.

"This chamber, Senhor Garrett, is one from the time of the rubber barons. Do you know of them—the rubber barons? I am told your man Ford styled this very room to his personal specifications. He was building a town as his namesake. Do you know of this man?"

"Of course. Henry Ford. He's famous."

Smiling yet shaking his head with disapproval, José said, "Of course you do. Your Mr. Henry Ford wanted *our* rubber."

This wouldn't be the last time Noah sensed a reprimand over "americanos" in Brazil.

José placed Noah's bag on the bed, then bowed at the waist. "I will show you the amenities, Senhor Garrett."

"Not necessary, José. I'll figure it out. I just need a little time to collect my thoughts, plan my day."

Upon leaving, José waved his index finger as Noah offered a gratuity. "No, senhor. You are a guest."

Once José had left, Noah started emptying his bag. The first thing he did was place a small silver-framed picture on the nightstand. Touching his fingers to his lips and then to the photograph, he grimaced.

"Now it begins," he whispered.

He unfolded a city map filled with names of streets he couldn't pronounce. The Teatro Amazonas—the opera house, circled in red and accentuated with an asterisk—stood out.

Chapter Thirteen

Most of us unknowingly spend some of our lives forming, dissecting, or reconfiguring our thoughts without bringing them to a conscious level. Lest these thoughts be lost forever, someone may make them conscious for us. Then we call it an epiphany.

MAP IN HAND, NOAH GARRETT stepped from the Hotel Santos into an intimidating, strange new world. As the hotel was located near the market, the scent of fish, rancid from the day before, was a discomforting prelude to what might lie ahead.

Once Noah located the Rua Dionísio da Silva, finding the opera house was easy. Although he expected it to be grand, its overpowering magnificence still came as a surprise. In awe, Noah walked the expansive perimeter of this iconic Renaissance-style theater, a prize located in one of the most foreboding jungles in the world. Its remarkable dome, embracing the colors of the national flag, stood impressive above what was once the most opulent city in the world.

Racked with pain and tethered to the most horrific day of his life, his mind nevertheless remained fixed as he chiseled a plan. A plan that, in some way, remained intimate to the cautionary, if not foreboding, edifice standing impressively on a distant hill. Neither exorbitant cost nor distraction would stand in his way.

To that end, and with the auspicious help of two thespian wannabes, he had already purchased tickets for the entire month's performances. Now he stopped at the calendar board to assure himself there were no changes. He would attend each performance not for its aesthetic value but to scrutinize the theater's clientele. The next event was three days hence, which allowed ample time to become familiar with the city.

Motivated by uncertainty, he found it reassuring there was but one person in this godforsaken city with whom he might identify. He pulled out Jack's card and proceeded to walk the streets in search of bric-a-brac and the closest thing he had to a friend.

Jack's shop was tucked unobtrusively between taller buildings in the middle of a block. Its neon marquee read, "Amazon Jack of All Trades."

Stepping through the metal front door was like entering a menagerie. Noah saw clutter, floor to ceiling, in this long, narrow room. Upon closer inspection, however, he could see an apparent order, with low-lying objects near the front and larger pieces ascending toward the rear. Dangling by ropes and twine from the ceiling was everything from bicycles to barber poles, bassinets to high chairs. There were even blowguns and darts—labeled "Curare Not Included." Glass cabinets contained neatly placed bibelots, likely positioned with a woman's touch.

Behind the cash register, barely visible, stood Flora. If she hadn't moved, she could have passed for just another sale item—which, Noah recalled, was exactly her station in life prior to meeting Jack.

She saw Noah long before he saw her. "Hello, americano," she called. Her dark skin, emblazoned by white teeth, distinguished her as she stood before a busy Portuguese tapestry. "You've come for souvenirs?"

Furrowing a pejorative brow, Noah was quick to dispel her inquiry. "No! I'm just trying to become acquainted with Jack's city. I kept his card. Your husband brought me to my hotel from the airport."

"*We*. It was *we* who brought you back from the airport. You're the Noah man. Yours is a biblical name. Easy to remember. I've read the Bible in English. Noah built the ark and saved his family. The animals too." She feigned an ingratiating wink, then smiled.

Noah thought her friendly, if not simple. And he certainly thought her naive, an impression fortified by her broad smile and almost childlike voice. He liked her nevertheless, and he could tell she liked him as well. He frequently relied on transference to gauge a relationship not established by time and experience.

"Jack isn't here now," Flora continued. "Can *I* help you?"

Assuming an indifferent pose, Noah looked about the room as he paid her little attention. "Ah . . . No," he uttered, distracted. His next reply was intentionally timid but unintentionally dismissive: "That is, I don't think so. I don't suppose you would know anything about the opera." Flora's initial response was an abbreviated frown quickly followed by a compliant smile. "Why of course. We go to the Teatro Amazonas frequently. Mostly for the orchestra. Its philharmonic prowess is renowned."

Noah found this dark-skinned Lilliputian's vocabulary both incongruous and surprising, especially when considering her pedigree. Even so, he gave her response only cursory attention, as his biased assumptions about her remained.

"I have photos of the Teatro Amazonas," Flora told Noah, "but this"—she stood aside, extending her arm to a piece of art resting on a decorative gilded easel—"this painting of our beautiful Teatro Amazonas is the prize. This is an original oil with a handcrafted frame made from the rubber tree. For me it represents a brief history of our city."

If not only to be compliant, Noah walked to the painting, passing his fingers along its frame. "Nice. But I'm really not interested in buying anything. I just wanted to ask your husband something about the opera house."

In actuality, Noah wanted to ask Jack about proper attire for an opera, never having attended one himself. Distressed, he now found himself on the waning end of an intellectual conundrum: as an implied sophisticate from Boston, he was reluctant to ask his question of someone he saw as a primitive from nowhere.

As he scanned the room with a quizzical ho-hum gaze, his countenance and words were telling. "So . . . when will Jack be coming back to his shop?"

Flora quickly stepped in front of her guest. "Sir, Mr. Noah Garrett," she said with emphatic enunciation, succinct in tone, "perhaps I can help you before my husband returns to *our* shop!"

Noah inadvertently rocked back on his heels. "Sorry. I didn't, ah, think," he stammered.

She took another step directly in front of Noah. "But you did—you *did* think!" Her words were vehement yet soft-spoken. "You think that because I am a native, I am unable to address your questions. Am I not correct? Mr. Garrett, I sense you are a nice man. Jack likes you, and that means I like you. That's how we are. But you are lost in a city and country of which you obviously know very little—perhaps nothing. I know, because Jack came to Brazil with the same misconceptions as you." She paused. "And I sense you are struggling with something you have brought here with you."

Noah was reduced to size. She was right. His condescending suppositions were inappropriate.

She was also right that he had brought something with him. He had become an affliction upon those he didn't even know. His pain was not only destroying him from within but also poisoning everyone he touched.

Dropping his chin, ashamed, he sank onto a wicker divan and held his head in his hands. Flora's dressing-down served as an awakening, a staggering blow to a quivering Noah Garrett.

Flora gently placed a hand on his shoulder. "Remember what I said, Mr. Garrett. Jack likes you, and so do I." Kneeling in front of him, she looked up, taking his hands in hers. "Just what is it you're looking for?"

Hesitant, faltering, tremulous, he said, "I'm sorry, Mrs. . . ." He froze. "I don't even know your last name. I—"

Feeling his anguish, she stopped him midsentence. "It's Morris. My name is Flora Morris, and I'm married to Jack Morris. As I said, he was like you when he came to Manaus. But in part, or perhaps only, because of me, he has learned about my country—now his country. He has learned more than most people might choose to learn in a lifetime. He knows this city, like this," she said, smiling as she traced a finger across the palm of her hand.

Flora's demeanor was gentle and assuring, welcoming Noah not only into her home but her heart as well. As if liberated for the first time since Jessie's death, he emptied his soul to this mite of a woman he didn't even know. He shared his narrative in its entirety. The catharsis was long overdue, a fulcrum from which he might once again become whole.

When he was done, he slowly leaned back in his chair and let out a deep sigh as he wiped tears from his eyes and tried to stop sobbing. Then he emitted an uncontrolled, blithering chuckle. Reaching out, he placed his hands on her cheeks, thanked her, and smiled for the first time since warding off the dangers of aces and eights.

"Thank *you*, Mr. Noah," Flora said, her voice velvet soft and reassuring. "Thank you for revealing a man in whom

I see both depth and substance. You are a real man, Mr. Noah. I assure you, you are in no way diminished by your tears. You have my respect." She took his hands in hers again. "Life is a relative experience. We cannot have a true appreciation for anything without seeing and feeling all that life offers. Now, what you do with it is up to you. Becoming whole and being whole are two separate things. Time can be your friend, perhaps?"

A booming voice came from behind a rack of dolls in the far corner of the room. Strutting to the front of the store, Jack looked invigorated and robust, if not a little sheepish.

"I came in through the back door, and I heard you talking," he said, nodding to Noah. "I didn't want to interrupt. But . . . yah, I heard everything you said about your girl, your search, the opera house. We can help you. As Flora said, we know the Teatro Amazonas." Jack beamed, his chest out. "The opera house quenches our appetite for the arts. We love the orchestra and the classical composers." He delivered a thumbs-up with a panoramic smile.

"We may live outside of your uppity-up world, but we're not ignorant," Jack continued. "You might be a doctor—your name was written on your carry-on, by the way—but you're just as clueless as I was before I came to what I thought was a godforsaken hole. What I learned is that this place gives life to the planet, and that this little woman here has wisdom beyond your wildest imagination." He smiled fondly at his wife. "The natives have something going for them that you and I don't have. The things you don't know limit you as a person. They limit you as a man." He then turned to Noah, with a smile. "If you want my help, I'll do everything I can for you. Why?" he asked before Noah could. "Because I see myself in you."

With clenched teeth and quaking lips, Noah looked at the couple. To his wonder, they had transformed—now mentors unto themselves. By convention, he had learned to quantify people by his initial impression. This experience with Jack and Flora Morris wasn't the first, nor would it be the last, time he was wrong.

And so his response came from a place infrequently visited. "Thank you, Amazon Jack Morris. And thank you, Mrs. Flora Morris. I've had many teachers in my life, but none with . . . with your message." His chest heaving, Noah took out a hankie and turned away.

"So tell me more about the man who brought you to Manaus," Jack said.

Noah drew a deep breath. "In the restaurant, when I first saw him—he was skinny, pixie-like, fragile, dressed in dark clothing. He looked plastic. I don't know his name, so I started calling him Knickknack."

Jack exchanged glances with Flora. "A skinny, plastic-appearing man?" he mused. "I know a man who could be your Knickknack. But he's far from fragile. He always wears a fedora, its brim turned up on one side." With that, Jack nodded. "I assure you, Dr. Noah Garrett, if I am right, you will meet this man—your Knickknack."

Noah clenched his fists.

If ever there were a portrait of vengeance wearing a smile, it was Noah Garrett.

Chapter Fourteen

Incipient

Evil as a cascade begets Evil

Self-sustaining without remorse

TWO YEARS PASSED. On an especially humid day, Caubi walked up to the porch of what had become his adopted home. The house was empty, as he knew it would be. Sabella was at the opera house arranging tickets and stacking playbills for the evening's performance. Abilio, a teetering Faust, was off selling both his soul and the lumber plundered from his beloved land.

Alone, Caubi had time and space to bask in the success of his devious enterprises. Abilio's lumber sales coupled with remuneration from Caubi's harvesting of "alluvial diamonds" was—by intent—barely enough to pay Sabella's tuition and ward off creditors. It was a scheme tooled and managed under the surreptitious eye of the man known as Bento Cardoso, the financier who held the purse strings for the family Almeida.

A tethered puppet, a man transformed, Abilio was beginning to fray. Paralyzed and plagued by remorse, he had become a liability. He often sat alone at the mission, fondling his beads while staring at his wife's picture. Not infrequently, Abilio also meandered through the port, watching with apprehension as a select crew prepared for their morning journey to the waters leading to his land. As far as he understood in his despair and naivete, the crew was having less and less success in sifting a lucrative diamond harvest.

The leaf was turning, soon to fall.

As Abilio watched the men prepare to embark one morning, Caubi walked up from behind. Moving himself alongside Abilio, he placed a consoling arm around the man's shoulder.

The time was ripe.

As if choreographed, Caubi stepped forward, turning to face his malleable friend. He grasped both of Abilio's tremulous hands.

"Abilio, Abilio, Abilio—my gracious landlord," Caubi began with a genteel and caressing tone. "I can see by the troubled look on your face that you have come to realize my strained ability to dredge for diamonds. The work is beginning to tax my men. But you needn't worry. For now, just as in the past, your lovely daughter will continue to receive her remittance."

Abilio's face flushed. He looked at the man he knew as Bento as if struck by an epiphany. An overabundant smile suddenly transformed his sullen face.

"I can help." He flexed his arm and pointed to his bicep. "I'm strong. See. Feel."

Caubi couldn't have scripted a better invitation. Forehead to forehead now, he firmly placed his hands on the old man's shoulders.

"Of course. You must accompany me to the site." As if leading a toddler, he grasped Abilio's hand and continued. "Come. There's work to be done. My boat is ready. Are *you* ready?"

Posed as a tantalizing question, there was but one answer. Abilio jumped into the skiff. Sitting at the bow, he looked once again at his biceps. He imagined his strength would serve the operation well.

All the while, Caubi watched with his eyebrows raised, cheeks puffed, and head shaking. He could only imagine the cockamamy world in which Abilio was living. Caubi reached beneath his own seat, fingered the contents of his bag, and smiled.

They motored over the black water. As they neared the hillside with crosses, Caubi became especially ceremonious and solemn.

"En route, we will pay homage to your departed wife. The love you show for your dear departed wife touches me deeply," he intoned. "Thank you for sharing that with me."

From Abilio's perspective, these words were ingratiating, as if delivered from a pulpit.

From Caubi's perspective, they were pernicious, as if tightening a noose.

Abilio stretched out his arms and pointed both index fingers toward the stern. "Bento, you are a man of your word." More than ever, he was convinced that his friend understood his grief, his need to share the loneliness he felt in the absence of his beloved Lucia.

Before disembarking at the burial site, Caubi coddled a smirk, slung his bag over his shoulder, dipped his head, and then gestured politely for Abilio to lead the way. Both men walked slowly to the top of the sandy hill, with Caubi a few steps behind.

Kneeling in front of the wooden marker, Abilio crossed himself and mumbled prayers as his chest began to heave.

Caubi reached into his bag. The trees muffled the piercing echo of the single riveting blast.

Calmly, Caubi nestled the gun in a stiffened hand then assembled the remaining contents of his duffel next to the grave. Before stepping back into his skiff, he turned, looked up the hill, and flicked a sarcastic salute.

"Perfect."

He tossed his empty bag into the back of the boat, brushed off his pants, and repositioned his hat.

"Perfect. Just fucking perfect."

Sabella didn't initially appreciate the fact that her father didn't return home that evening. She always retired early the night before an opening performance. Ticket sales and brochure distribution required her to leave home well before dawn the next morning. She assumed both her tenant and her father were still sleeping as she left her home.

When she returned later that evening, however, she informed João that her father was not home and that his bed hadn't been slept in. With guarded skepticism, she assumed he had remained with friends after a night of what had gradually transitioned into excessive drinking.

Later, when her father's body was found next to her mother's riverside grave, there was no one more consoling than João. As João explained, Abilio had been unable to face the travesties he had committed. He saw suicide as his only option. His note left no doubt, though Sabella could not bring herself to even look at what was written.

Although Sabella's financial needs were summarily met, João remained skeptical. This Bento Cardoso dressed in fine clothes and wore a large diamond like the ones he claimed he harvested near the Almeida land.

Why would such a man of the town choose to live an unlikely existence as a tenant in a small home? Could he really be harvesting diamonds? If not, then what was he harvesting? Where did the payments for Sabella's tuition come from? What—or who—did this man want?

For João, nothing made sense. The questions brought him to a breaking point. He needed answers.

With Sabella at work and Abilio now passé, the house should have been empty when Caubi returned from the Rio Negro, carrying a duffel over his shoulder. However, the front door was open.

Suspicious, Caubi crept to a side window. Looking directly into his room, he angrily shook his head. *Goddamn. I knew it.* There was João, extracting an identical duffel from beneath the bed, where Caubi had placed it the night before.

Caubi gritted his teeth as João opened the duffel to reveal the powder-filled cellophane bags inside. As he carefully replaced the bag, the look of enlightenment and determination was plain to see.

Caubi shifted position so he could see João exit the house and vault off the front porch. A pair of leather leggings were tucked beneath his arm. He was headed to the forest. Caubi watched as João's Greek fisherman cap disappeared down the street.

With João now out of sight, Caubi darted inside to retrieve the duffel before racing to the port. With the *Fuga* loading for Boston, Richter would be waiting for this, the last of his cargo.

There was no swagger as Caubi ran up the gangplank, dropping the duffel at Helmut Richter's feet. Sure enough, the German stood impatiently, arms akimbo, toe tapping.

"We have a small problem," Caubi said. He pointed at the duffel. "The bitch's meddling boyfriend saw this. He knows what's up." Though marginally compromised, Caubi nonetheless managed a sinister smile. "I'm sure he's on his way to the plantation now. He knows the route. I'll take Fatty's boat." Hesitant, he added, "I . . . I'll need your piece. I had to leave mine with the old man."

With a look of disgust, Richter glared at the man who was now his nemesis. Slamming his heel to the deck, he growled as he turned and left to retrieve his gun from his cabin. Returning with a vintage Luger, he shoved the holstered weapon and a box of ammunition into Caubi's gut.

"It's been vis me since Dunkirk. The last time I saw you fire a weapon, you blew your fat friend's face half off and ruined mein dinner. I'll vant it back." Under his breath, he added an intentionally audible, "*Schweinehund.*"

He snatched the duffel from the deck, clicked his heels, and walked away, chin up, in preparation for his departure.

Wasting no time, Caubi ran several blocks to the public side of the port. He hurriedly boarded the boat formerly owned by an obese half-jawed drunk who some said met his demise choking to death on a fish bone—though Caubi knew he had been eating pudding at the time.

For a man usually in control, Caubi was now desperate as he made his way upriver, motoring around and between larger vessels. It would take one hour to reach the tributary and another to locate what he now called *his* terra firma. His horticultural gift was at risk.

He had always instructed his sentries to dispatch any intruders by claiming the property was government land. But he knew João wouldn't accept the ploy. Pounding his fist on the gunwale of the boat, Caubi hoped the problem would be solved before his arrival. Messy things had to be eliminated. He didn't like messy things.

The canopy of trees cast long, angular shadows as the sun made its descent in the west. It would be dark soon. Whatever needed to be done would have to occur soon. Getting lost in this infernal hell wasn't an option.

Looking across the river, he could see a flock of greater yellow-headed vultures circling the small group of crosses barely visible on the hillside. King vultures were already on the ground.

Abilio was just another meddling bastard. Served him right.

He passed his fingers over the handle of the cold steel he had in his pocket. Removing it from the holster, he could see it was already loaded.

The Nazi pig doesn't miss a trick.

Two hours later, as expected, Caubi approached the rivulet abutting the plantation. Also as anticipated, he saw João's boat beached on the shore.

Caubi disembarked and started along the footpath. Before long, he was greeted from behind with a rifle barrel thrust between his shoulder blades.

"*Pare*," a man commanded.

As instructed, Caubi stopped, then turned slowly. "Robby," he said to his lead sentry. "I trained you well. It's me—Bento. You wouldn't want to shoot the hand that feeds you." Smiling, he cocked his hat to the back of his head before patting Robby on both cheeks. "See? It's me."

"I'm so sorry, Senhor Cardoso. I didn't know it was you." Robby's eyes sheepishly dropped for a moment, but he quickly snapped to attention. "We caught a man on your land. As instructed, we said this was government land and he must leave. He said that was not true. When we insisted, he said it was a lie. He might be with the *polícia*?"

"No. But almost as bad."

Sidestepping overhanging limbs, the pair made their way toward a clearing.

"He's in the cage," Robby said. "Says he knows what we're doing. Says he knows you. I thought it would be best to tell you this before . . . you know . . . we took action."

Caubi nodded. "It's good you waited. I'll speak with him. We must learn what his bitch knows."

Taking the lead, Robby shuffled ahead while parting branches for his master, a man he knew from experience could, when irritated, be ruthless beyond reproach.

After opening the razor-wire gate, they approached a bamboo cage so small it would not allow even a small man to stand. João squatted inside, his forehead pressed against the vertical bars. Blood was spattered across his face. His bruised eyes fluttered open long enough to recognize the man he knew as Bento.

It was apparent an interrogation had already begun—without the master's consent. Fearful he had overstepped his authority, Robby clasped his hands beneath his chin in anticipation of rebuke. He could do no more than whimper an explanation.

"He—he was saying things against you, Senhor Cardoso. We made him stop. He is not badly hurt, though. He can still talk."

As if consoling a stray dog, Caubi gently patted his vassal on the head. "That's okay, Robby. Just so long as he can still talk."

Caubi squatted so he could look in the cage at João. He clasped his hands between his knees, shaking his head.

"Tsk-tsk-tsk . . . Now, what do we have here? You've been a very bad boy, haven't you, João? You always doubted it was diamonds, didn't you? Then you started pushing your sniffy little nose where it didn't belong. How foolish."

Now on his knees, João faced the ground. His chest rose and fell in rapid succession, hyperventilating as an ill attempt to gain a satisfying breath.

Leering at his prisoner, Caubi rattled the bamboo cage. "Look at me, you sniveling little man! All bent over in your new home. You might be strong when outside of the bamboo, but from where I am, you look very small. Don't you, college boy?"

Suddenly steeling himself, João willed his lips to stop quivering. He slowly looked up and simply said, "You pig." With tears lining his cheeks, he took a deep breath, seeking resolve. He then nodded his head and, as if in defiance, accepted the reality of his plight.

"Now, how important is your girlfriend, college boy? Don't you realize that without me, she and everything she owns would belong to the bank? My question for you is a simple one: What does your little queen bee know? Think carefully, my friend. You do understand that two lives depend on what you say. Possibly—yours and, of course, hers."

Caubi leaned back a bit, rocking on his heels. "Or perhaps you do not believe me. Do you remember Abilio? Oh, of course you do. You know he is no longer with us. He was on his knees, crying. Like you, he became a problem. He was crumbling. Soon to break. That is when I put a gun to his head."

With a quick jerk, João stared in horror at the man the Almeidas had allowed into their home, their lives. After a controlled, time-altering pause, he smiled. His fate was no longer in question.

"You're beneath a pig," he said. "You're a coward."

Caubi chuckled. "Look at you. Your feeble words cannot harm me. It is a shame you were not privy to this truth about Abilio before you put your nose where it didn't belong. So, how does the truth make you feel now, college boy? Do you want your opera pigeon to be next? You must tell me the truth, or the lovely Sabella will meet the same circumstance as the man who was to be your father-in-law."

With nostrils flared and both hands shaking the bamboo bars, Caubi now raised his voice. "Do you understand, college boy? *What does she know?*"

With that, João's momentary strength shattered. His response was once again unrestrained. "Nothing, Mr. Bento!" he cried. He reached through the bamboo bars, pleading, as he attempted to grasp his captor's hands. "She knows nothing. She receives your payments at the opera house and asks no questions. She's never doubted that it comes from the sale of diamonds. Only I know. I became suspicious when Abilio—when—" He found himself unable to finish the sentence. "So I went to your room today, and that's when I knew. I came straight here. I swear, Sabella knows nothing of this. She remains loyal to you."

His begging hands now clasped as if in prayer, João looked up at the man he still—even in this time of revelations—believed was named Bento Cardoso. Tears made streaks as they washed the congealed blood from his cheeks.

"She knows nothing, I swear!" he repeated.

Caubi turned slowly from the cage and smiled at Robby. In anticipation, Robby stood back a few feet, observing the unfolding scene through clenched teeth.

"He is telling the truth," the master said to the sentry.

Reaching into his pocket, he looked back at João. "Yes, you tell the truth. Your crying will stop now."

Raising his eyebrows and licking his lips, he stepped toward the cage and raised the gun, firing a single shot.

"You see. Now it has stopped." He turned toward his sentry once again. "Robby, the river waits. It's hungry. Feed it."

Chapter Fifteen

Side by side as bedfellows, need seduced by deception breeds naivete.

THE AIR WAS UNUSUALLY THICK as the afternoon sun pierced a single low-hanging cloud. In the distance, however, barely visible over the tree line, the sky was becoming black. It was all in keeping with the local climate, generally described as hot and wet.

The shimmering sun cast an eerie gray hue as Sabella paced on the porch. From time to time, she would stop and strain her ears, hoping she would hear the hum of João's motorcycle. She never heard it. She checked her watch to see if she might be mistaken about the time. She wasn't.

João was always punctual. And when a punctual person is late, it means something is wrong. Already tormented by the lurid description of her father's death, Sabella couldn't help but feel conflicted and alone.

She stepped inside to check the clock above the stove; it read the same as her watch. João had given her the watch two years previous, about the time the man she knew as Bento had arrived.

Sabella could recall her father's words about their new tenant: "He's a blessing. He answered my prayers."

Folding her hands, she looked up, whispering, "Now, please let him answer mine. Perhaps he knows where João is." She then glanced at her father's picture on the mantle. "Sad. You'll never realize the gift Bento brought to our home." Unwittingly, she made a vacillating grimace.

Peering through the window, she was instantly relieved. "Bento," she said aloud. His mere proximity served to allay her fears. With arms extended, she ran down the steps. As if reaching for a lifeline, she grasped his hands.

"João hasn't returned," she blurted. Then she quickly added, "It's silly of me, I know, to worry. But why hasn't he called? He's always on time. It's probably nothing, right?" Hers were questions orchestrating an answer.

With a sympathetic smile, Caubi looked at her desperate and pleading face. "I'm sure you're right—it's probably nothing."

Wrapping his arms around her shoulders, his was a comforting embrace. As though she were a child, he swayed Sabella from side to side. With her head tucked into his shoulder, he could have been humming her a lullaby. He was in control.

Rolling his eyes, he looked up, measuring every word with purpose. "Though I do understand your fears. You see, I spoke with João earlier today. He was troubled by rumors of loggers moving barges onto the Rio Negro. He said they may have entered the river from your father's—I mean, *your* land." She was her father's heir, after all. He continued. "João said he was going to look into the matter. He didn't say how."

Releasing her, he stepped back, extending one hand while elevating her chin with the other.

"If he doesn't return soon, I could ask his friends at the wharf if they have any ideas. Would you like me to do that . . . for you?" Palms up, he stretched his hands as if extending an offering.

Her enthusiastic response was as anticipated, almost choreographed. "Of course," she said, nodding vigorously. "Thank you."

Her consent was nourishment for an insatiable palate.

Sabella drew a deep breath. Although feeling marginally relieved, she remained emotionally tormented. Still needing his physical presence, she was now abundantly eager to gratify. "Please let me do something while we wait for João. Tea, perhaps?"

The smiling chameleon was more than a lecher. He was Rasputin-like, with commanding strength. Omnipotent. His thoughts were staged now. One of his mottoes: *People see what they wish to see. They feel what they wish to feel.*

He placed an indulging hand on the small of her back, ushering her inside. He sat at the kitchen table, leaning back, knees apart with his forearms across his lap. He wrangled his thumbs, watching as she prepared the tea.

Although distressed, her movements remained steady and, to him, enticing.

People are always at their weakest and most vulnerable when they are needy, he thought. Rhythmically, he began tapping his fingers on the table. *Magnificent. There is a lot more to this woman than I thought.*

Waiting for the water to heat, she sat across the table from him. Her entire body was pulled tight with worry.

With a look of authoritative assurance, Caubi got up and walked behind her. Placing one hand on her shoulder, he used the other to gently tease her hair as he leaned toward her ear.

The image was telling—revealing his true nature. But Sabella would not have recognized the spectacle had she been holding a looking glass.

"Sabella, perhaps we should share tea another time. Let me go to the wharf. I'll see what can be done. You should stay here. Try to relax."

Up until that moment, he had generally addressed her as "senhorita," as the use of her first name would have implied a familiarity inappropriate between tenant and landlord. But this time, his use of her name repositioned him into a dynamic of ownership. Preoccupied and distraught, she was unaware of the transition.

Employing a subtle emotional dagger, his next words were select: "Look—the skies are becoming dark. Our ray of sunshine is about to leave us. I'll go to look for João now. I'm sure there's an explanation."

Sabella couldn't be sure if his words were reassuring or foreboding—and he knew it.

He passed his hand across the back of her neck as he left the room. She was comforted, but again none the wiser.

Hearing the front door close, Sabella was once again alone with her thoughts. Searching for solace, she moved about the room repositioning photographs as she recalled the day João had danced her down the front steps onto the lawn, delighted they had found a new tenant for the spare room. She mustered a smile and shook her head. She mused about how different her boarder had been back then. Cocky, with a quizzical, over-the-shoulder look.

She also recalled how João had always viewed Bento with skepticism. He reminded her, on more than one occasion, of the way the new tenant had held her by the waist as the three of them rode to and from the bistro.

Lost within herself and blinded by the fear that something had happened to João, she gave no thought to how strange it was for such recollections to surface at this time. Rather, all her thoughts centered on a reverberating conundrum for which she had no answer.

Jagged chains of lightning ripped through dreaded black clouds that approached from the east. With her mind intangibly conflicted, Sabella stood, wringing her hands. As much as she tried to suppress the thought, she feared that not every cloud had a silver lining. A calamitous roll of thunder echoed across the Amazon basin.

Less than an hour later, Sabella was surprised to see the man called Bento suddenly reappear. Without a word, he took her by the arm and led her to the settee. Wearing a somber mask of compassion, he knelt in front of her.

"I . . . ," he began with willful hesitation. "I'm not sure how to present this. You see, João ventured alone on the river . . . hours ago. The dockworkers said he left in haste, without preparing for this sudden bad weather. He hasn't returned."

Watching her already-fragile composure become even more compromised, he gently stroked the tears from her cheeks with the back of his fingers.

"I have considered contacting the police," he began, his forehead furrowed, "but I fear they might only be interested in looking for a barge or large ferry. They would not consider searching for one man in a small boat. This time of year, the water has reached its zenith and has extended far into the forest."

Now sitting beside her, Caubi never lost sight of his boundaries. He positioned himself close yet just far enough away; he didn't want proximity mistaken for lasciviousness. Emotional manipulation was much more rewarding than carnal satisfaction. The latter was short lived—a lesson he had learned in his mother's home.

"I will, of course, gather my loyal workers as a search party." He carefully crafted the word selection and candor of his bifurcated message. It created the precise moment to caress her hand. "As we are losing the light of day, and with the unfortunate weather, maneuvering the river would put more people in peril. There are hundreds of islands upriver, and distinguishing them from the shoreline is impossible." He brushed her face again. "I feel it would be best to wait for the light of day."

Sabella looked down. "I know you're right. The river . . . the river can be dangerous." Her response was restrained. "We can wait and start tomorrow."

She knew the Rio Negro, and she knew João. The river was unforgiving. There were too many crosses along its banks, too many crosses where unknown adventurers had lost their way.

Sabella told herself how fortunate it was that this man from Rio de Janeiro had learned so much about the river. His knowledge would serve them well. He would find João.

Tomorrow.

Caubi rose to his feet. "I should retire for the night," he declared, bowing his head. "Tomorrow may be a long day," he added.

As he prepared to leave, he extended his hands and prayerfully clasped Sabella's, drawing her closer without physically touching her in any way that could be deemed inappropriate.

"I meant to tell you earlier, before . . ." He dramatically let his words fade. "The sale of your stones has been only somewhat lucrative lately." With a tip of his fedora, he turned and prepared to leave.

The implications of "only somewhat" served their purpose. If Sabella had been a reader of signs, she would have also noted his reference to the stones as *hers*. It was a pronoun used with purpose.

But then Caubi turned back, wearing a reassuring smile. "The envelopes will continue to follow each performance, though," he said.

Still ingratiating, he could now consume the rest of what had been Sabella Almeida, the Redeemer. But restraint would serve him well.

That night, in the comfort of his bed and with a contorted sense of resolve, Caubi listened as Sabella paced in the kitchen, outside of his door. Later, he listened as she wept—alone, in her bed. It was only his mind that wandered into her room.

An early riser, Caubi stepped into the kitchen, where Sabella was already drinking yesterday's tea. It was obvious she had slept in her clothes. Her eyes were red and swollen.

Caubi appeared contrite, sharing her burden.

Without a word, he took her hand, never releasing it as they walked to the port.

The *Fuga* having set sail, Richter's remaining minions were now Caubi's to command. These longshoremen harvested coca while Richter was at sea. As tagalongs from Rio, they knew the trade well. Collectively, they lived both sides of the equation—some were accomplished producers and others inveterate users. Some were euphoric, while others ground their teeth and sniffed, making it easy for the educated to differentiate on which side of the continuum they fell. Chattering speech, runny noses, and bruxism were the indelible monograms for habitual users.

Caubi assembled a search party, as none of these men had been informed of the true status of the man for whom they were searching. It was a facade orchestrated to perfection.

Sabella was pleased as she witnessed her tenant's authority. Three motorized dories, each carrying two men, readied to set off upstream, one on each side of the river. Meanwhile, the man she knew as Bento was centrally positioned, serving as a communication hub for the port and starboard boats. Standing at the bow, he was clearly in charge.

Before embarking, Caubi turned to the woman standing on the dock. "Sabella, you should go to the opera house," he said. "Work will be distracting. It will help you through a worrisome day." His rhetoric was designed to be comforting, but his real purpose was to leave her to sit in anguish, alone.

She nodded and, with an imperfect smile, extended a dire wave as the boats disappeared into the mist. The search party was in good hands.

She didn't know whether she should feel a sense of relief or guarded despair.

Returning to the ticket booth as instructed served its purpose. It was an imprecise distraction from an untenable day. The Teatro Amazonas was the home of the Amazonas Philharmonic, and its stage had been graced by dance, jazz, and the world's finest opera. It had been said that Enrico Caruso performed there.

For two years, the Teatro Amazonas had also housed performances by the multifaceted Caubi Tomayo. He would meet Sabella, exchange tickets for a manila envelope, and leave with a burly German captain.

Sabella's thoughts were a whirlwind. How fortuitous that a man such as Bento would grace her doorstep, not only to become her tenant but to assume the role of benefactor. João had initially thought the quest to find alluvial diamonds was preposterous. But Bento had proven him wrong.

Bento sold the diamonds to wealthy fashion plates in the United States. Sabella harbored contempt for these buyers. Nonetheless, she knew they made it possible for her to secure an education and retain her coveted land.

That is, Bento Cardoso made it possible. He had rescued her from despair in the past. Could he do it once again?

Sabella tried to hum the day away, waiting for word from Bento regarding the search. As a student of mythology, she clung to the last remaining remnant of Pandora's box—hope. She chose to believe an improbable yet not implausible scenario: To evade the storm, João had stayed the night with friends who lived on the river. After all, he knew many natives who lived a riparian existence far from the city, friends indigenous to the rain forest.

Late that evening, well into Rossini's *The Italian Girl in Algiers*, a loud creak shook Sabella from her abstracted escape. The large central door opened. She stiffened as Bento entered. He extended his arms as if making an offering. In his hand, she saw a Greek fisherman's cap.

"I—I—I don't know what to say," he said with well-crafted stuttering. "I believe this is João's. We found it . . . in his boat. It was overturned on the riverbank near a violent whirlpool."

Although the band was missing its decorative braid, she recognized the cap. She took it slowly from Bento.

When she turned the cap over, she saw João's name. She had stitched it in the band when she gifted him the cap.

Her imaginary scenario had come to an end.

Passing her finger through a gaping hole in the back of the cap, she looked questioningly up at Bento.

His patented look ranged somewhere between a smirk and grimace. Sabella chose to see the grimace.

"As you can see, there is a tear in the cap," he said quietly. "And this—perhaps blood?" He pointed to a crimson streak. "I'm afraid he fell from the boat and was consumed by the current. He must have struck his head. We are all convinced that is what happened," he added, knowing that any news, especially sorrowful, is legitimized by numbers. "In all her fury, the black waters of the Rio Negro have taken him from us. We returned his boat to its berth."

Reaching out, he drew her close, sharing her loss. Endearment was his finale.

This man she called Bento was the buoy that kept her afloat. Led like a pull toy—just like her father before her—she had no options. The envelopes would keep coming. Her tuition was paid, and more than the bank was satisfied. He was the only man in Sabella's life.

For now.

Chapter Sixteen

We see that which we wish to see, until circumstance opens our eyes. Pavlovian, perhaps.

TEMPERED BY THE RAIN, the night had cooled. Slickened streets cast a silvery sheen. The Teatro Amazonas—brilliantly lit, majestic, and grandiose—illuminated the night sky. Attempting to evade the evening mist, patrons scurried along the marble walk leading to the vestibule of this nineteenth-century masterpiece.

Across the street, Noah stood at the Praça de São Sebastião. Black and white tiles beneath his feet formed an undulating mosaic representing the meeting of the waters: the Rio Negro and the Solimões. His eyes were set on Jack, who stood at a distance with his collar pulled over his ears.

Jack, in turn, watched as people jockeyed their way into the grand building. Although visibility was limited, he would surely recognize the frame and strutting gait of the man Noah called Knickknack. Once he spied him, he would give Noah the signal.

Imbued with swagger, Caubi made his way to the front of the imposing, lofty edifice via a curved stairway embellished with rose-colored balusters. He was accompanied, as he often was, by an unshaven European man wearing an oilskin slicker over what appeared to be a peacoat. Though inconsistent with the Amazonian climate, this man's attire was nonetheless tolerable for one made resolute from the rigors of a sordid past.

Stopping at the top rail, Caubi turned to look down at the converging crowd as they wound their way up the walkway. He recognized the same old faces—recidivist clappers whose lives revolved around this thespian scene.

Offset from the advancing throng, however, one man was standing still. Conspicuous.

Caubi could not quite make out the man's face, but he could see the man make a nodding gesture in a far-off direction. After doing so, the man canted his head, then looked directly at Caubi at the top of the facade.

It was clearly a signal of acknowledgment. And it didn't go unnoticed by the man being acknowledged.

Caubi's eyes darted about the plaza, trying to locate whoever had been on the other side of the signal. It was impossible—streams of people coursed by, not unlike the rivers the black and white tiles symbolized.

With a slow and contemplative elevation of his chin, Caubi pooched his cheeks. After a disgruntled jerk of his head, he took his male companion by the arm, spoke directly into his ear, and walked hurriedly into the theater.

From his position near the Abertura dos Portos monument, Noah had followed Jack's signal to the man standing at the top rail. And now his brain pummeled with castigating thoughts. He could once again hear angry voices filtering through a lattice of bougainvillea, intertwined with blood spewing over a checkered cloth and a perfect world coming to an end.

Noah talked to himself through clenched teeth: "Goddamn dirty rotten bastard." Fulminating, he pounded a closed fist into his other hand.

Immediately walking to the far side of the Abertura dos Portos monument, Jack was eager to join his waiting friend.

"Well, what do you think?" Jack asked. "Did you get a good look at him too?"

Noah leaned forward, his hands now resting heavily against the European facade, his head slumped down between his arms. With his chest heaving, he spoke. "It's the hat—the way he wears that confounded hat. It's him. It's Knickknack, that miserable bastard."

In that instant, transformed, the man once of purposeful direction and cultivated intent ceased to exist.

Forbearing, Jack now crouched at Noah's side and looked up at him. "You're sure? You're positive—no doubts?"

Noah stood and quickly turned, pressing his finger directly into Jack's chest. "Not a doubt in my mind. That's him."

"Well, you do seem damn sure." Jack checked his watch. "The performance will last two hours. We should wait across the street in the café, then return later for a better look when the crowd is leaving."

Glaringly introspective and with a tightened jaw, Noah said nothing as he followed Jack to the café. Once positioned at a table near a curbside window, Jack took the liberty of ordering two coffees.

Expressionless, Noah stared across the street, fixated on the Teatro Amazonas glistening in the evening rain. He stared at the splendor before him while he contemplated the task at hand. Transfixed, speechless, and deep in thought, he massaged his temples and muttered like an animal pondering its prey. Simply sitting and waiting two hours could have been disquieting, but it wasn't.

Something—someone—had changed.

And then suddenly, as if carried by a diaphanous wind, Noah displayed a sense of calm. He had been transported to another place, another time. Smiling, he now vicariously watched as Jessie displayed her coquettish grin, golden hair, and a come-hither wink as she played prankster with the man she loved. The world was right.

Seeing this perplexing shift play across Noah's face, Jack shook the young man's arm. "Where in the hell *are* you?" His eyes were a mix of confusion and concern.

Dashed back to reality, Noah slammed his fist on the table. "I know who I am, where I am, and what I have to do!"

In that instant, Jack witnessed the transition of Noah Garrett. There was no genial smile of satisfaction. Instead, Jack saw a pernicious grin of sinister anticipation. He scrutinized a man altering before his very eyes.

"You're different," Jack said quietly. "You look . . . well . . . almost satisfied."

Noah turned from the window, robotically and slowly, as though looking through Jack. "Yeah. It'll happen. Not sure just how. But it will. Count on it."

Nothing more was said as Noah looked down, tracing his finger around the face of his watch. But only moments later, he sat up and blurted, "I've crossed it. The Rubicon." He slammed his cup on the table. "Back to the opera house, now!"

Jack jolted back in his chair, holding out his palms in abeyance. "Okay, my friend." An eyebrow raised. "You *are* still my friend . . . ?"

"Of course."

Then, without hesitation, Noah was up, leading a brisk pace to the Teatro Amazonas.

The rain had stopped, leaving a dank stillness in the air. Upon entering the building, they could hear the finale, a drawn-out aria, during which the operatic plot was resolved.

For Noah, however, the composition was but an overture. The true aria had yet to be written.

Following a loud round of applause, the massive doors opened, and a satisfied audience filed through the atrium. Loquacious, still clapping, they bounded toward the exit.

With a flair of arrogance, the man with the fedora sauntered across the vestibule, arm in arm with his incongruent friend.

The moment Knickknack came into his field of vision, Noah was ignited with uncontrolled déjà vu. He once again heard the discontent of foreign voices and saw blood spewing across a checkered tablecloth.

Without forethought, he lurched forward like a ravenous beast—and in doing so collided with a woman, knocking her to her knees and sending the contents of her purse across the marble floor.

Even though he leaned forward to help gather the strewn items, Noah paid little attention to the woman herself. His head swiveled and bobbed, trying unsuccessfully to keep eyes on the man with the fedora.

On her knees, irate, and with piercing defiance, the woman looked directly into Noah's eyes. "*Gringo!* Look where you're going. You're barbaric and rude. You disgust me!" She never took her eyes off Noah, even as she discreetly placed a manila envelope back into her purse.

Oblivious to her diatribe, Noah scrambled back to his feet and scanned the room. In his hands, he fumbled with a playbill, a tube of lipstick, and a string of beads he didn't recognize as a rosary.

"Damn it. He's gone." Looking around and through the woman, he asked, "Did you see him—the guy with the hat?"

The woman shook her fist, then snatched the items from his hands. "*Desgraçado americano.*"

Forcing the remaining articles into her purse, she wheeled around, darted to the teller's booth, and disappeared.

Noah ran to the mezzanine's outer rail. Jack was close behind. But the opera house was now empty, and the quarry was nowhere to be seen. Scanning the plaza, the men stood in silence.

Then they heard a thud and a loud crash, followed by a blood-curdling scream.

A crowd quickly gathered along the Rua Marçal.

Moments earlier, Noah had been a man unhinged—yet one preconditioned and pliable enough to still be compelled by the shriek of resonating anguish. He had but one requisite response: he ran down the steps and parted the mass of people lining the rain-slickened street.

He could see only the tennis shoes of a child protruding from beneath a car. A young woman, hands to her face, choked out agonal screams as motionless onlookers gawked from the curb.

On his knees, Noah reached beneath the car, gently pulling the child into view. He held the boy close to his body. Given Noah's occupation, this was not an unfamiliar sight, but he was nonetheless sickened by what he saw. Bloody gray tissue pulsated from the child's ears, nose, and mouth. Ashen, he had already assumed the cast of a corpse. That which had once harbored child's play and whimsical pranks was now reduced to tapioca-like ooze seeping between Noah's fingers. His head was cradled in Noah's hands; it was obvious the child's skull had been crushed.

The young woman collapsed to her knees. "*Meu menino, meu menino.*"

Pleading, she took Noah's arm. Looking directly into his eyes, with hands clasped, she pleaded for him to be something he couldn't be—the savior of her child.

"*Oh, Deus. Por favor, ajude meu menino!*" she wailed.

From behind, a woman's soft voice whispered into Noah's ear. "She's asking you to help him."

Rather than turn toward the voice, Noah looked directly into the child's eyes. "But I can't help."

"Why?" the voice asked.

Almost apologetically, he said, "Because he's . . . he's dead."

Noah now looked up. With a look of stuttering perplexity, he realized the woman whispering in his ear was the same woman he had dashed to her knees in the vestibule. This same woman raised a staggered brow as she looked down at a man now on his knees. They were both momentarily drawn back several frames in time, to a moment when their established predilections had been reaffirmed.

Out of his element, Noah then turned, his only option but to embrace the sobbing mother, bowing his head to conceal his tears.

The emergency room was his professional turf. There, he expected to witness tattered bodies. There, however, the bodies were positioned on padded gurneys, partially hidden in white sheets, with faces already cleansed by the receiving nursing staff.

But seeing this boy here, at the scene of an accident, was different. Here, there was no time to prepare for a discussion with a grieving parent. Noah felt inept as he shared the mother's pain.

Though share it he did. As he looked down at his outstretched, bloody palms, the lancinating rush of empathy transported him to a corner table in an Argentine restaurant, where one life ended, and another changed forever.

The woman from the lobby took a step back and observed. How unusual to see a man turn from a specious villain one minute to a compassionate yet devitalized guardian angel the next. In the vestibule, perhaps she had seen that which she wanted to see. Regardless of her fated perception, inexplicably, this was not the same man.

Noah stayed with the mother and the dead child until the ambulance arrived. As the ambulance drove off, Noah wiped his bloody hands on his shirt and returned to the curb, where Jack now stood with the woman from the opera house.

"Noah," Jack said gently, "this woman works at the admissions window at the opera house. She's the woman you ran into. Her name is Sabella. I've been speaking with her."

If the carnage Noah had just witnessed were etchings from hell, then the sight standing before him was redemption in the form of an angel. He was strangely captivated by her ebony hair, brown eyes, and delicate auburn-copper skin.

Sabella tucked her chin while turning her head to the side, as if to evaluate him from different angles. "You don't appear to be the same man I saw in the theater. You . . . I mean . . . ," she began, fumbling for words. "You are like two people."

Noah looked directly at Sabella. Holding both open hands out in front of him, as if making a plea, he tried to establish his point. "But . . . but . . . I'm not. I'm just . . . me." His appeal was stammering but resolute.

Yet unrecognized within the very substance of this singular being, an ideological battle was taking place—a subliminal craving for an identity.

In that moment, Noah had a similar realization: he did not recognize this to be the same contemptuous woman he'd encountered in the opera house, the one who had chastised him with vile speech and scorn.

Conflicted, they both struggled for stable ground on which to establish a semblance of civility. Both, as if by serendipity, felt an apology seemed in order.

Words tumbled out of Noah in a jumble. "I'm sorry. In the corridor—I didn't see you. I didn't mean to—" As if interrupting himself, he suddenly looked at Jack. "We should go," he said, already turning.

Sabella stepped in front of Noah. "No, please," she insisted. She was equally as awkward. "It is I who should apologize."

They stood frozen for a moment, then gave nods and attempted smiles, guardedly congenial as they made amends.

Obligingly indelicate and cautiously terse, Jack took each of them by the arm.

"Wait a minute. There's something both of you must understand." He looked at Noah first. "She knows the two guys who walked out of the opera house. She was, well, sort of . . . with them. You didn't see her because you were obsessed with your guy, Knickknack."

Jack then turned to Sabella. "Senhorita, you and Noah here share more than a rude encounter and a spilled purse. It's that guy. It's *him* you share. You two have to talk." Jack gestured down at the blood-splattered street. "But this isn't the time—certainly not the place. Both of you, come to my home. Tomorrow."

Sabella, still at odds with all that had transpired, stood her ground. "No, come to mine." Now she was decidedly insistent. "It . . . it would be best if you came to mine."

She pulled a playbill and a pen from her purse, then wrote her address. With an inquiring look and deep sigh, Sabella touched Noah's blood-stained shirt with one hand and offered him the playbill with the other. Saying nothing, she looked directly at him.

Shaking her head with a countenance of disbelief, she turned and left.

Chapter Seventeen

Concealed within every person, passionate opposing suppositions exist. Inclinations, when jarred from their hollows, become dichotomies exposed.

IT MADE LITTLE SENSE—accepting a white-faced foreigner into her home the night after he impetuously dashed her to the floor yet also caressed, with blood-soaked hands, a grief-stricken mother of a dead child. Hatefulness gilded in compassion didn't make sense.

Hearing a knock on the door, Sabella looked up to see the silhouettes of two men peering through the screen. One man was the conundrum, and the other an apparent transplant who had the audacity to say she had something to learn from them. Something about the man she knew as Bento.

She swept a quick glance about the living room to make sure all was in order. Then, with shoulders back and chin up, Sabella walked with assurance to the door.

Wielding rancorous confidence, she ushered them in. Stone faced, she glared at both men. There were no formalities or introductions.

Jack and Noah immediately felt like unwanted guests. They looked at each other but said nothing, sharing a cloak of restraint.

Noah eyed the room. The drapes were drawn, and the filtered light cast a pastel-amber hue throughout the room—orderly, somber, and mournful. The setting spawned a mood not unlike that of a mausoleum.

Rigidly pointing to a settee, Sabella was incisive and curt. "Sit," she directed.

Both men bumped into each other before assuming their designated positions. Jack did all he could to suppress a laugh. Noah bit his tongue.

"Do you know who those people are?" Sabella asked. She pointed once again, drawing the men's attention to a trio of framed photos on a corner table. "Of course not," she said obtrusively before they had a chance to answer.

Noah and Jack knew to remain silent. It was as though they had entered a play midway through the first act, not knowing whether it was drama or comedy. There was no option but to sit and listen.

"To you, they might be meaningless," she continued as she walked to the corner table. "They're not, gentlemen. If that is what you are—*gentlemen*. They're memories. They're people who gave me life and something for which to live. They made me not only who I was but who I've become."

Noah stiffened, then he leaned toward Jack. "I don't have to listen to this garbage," he mumbled under his breath. His muscles twitched as if to stand.

Jack put a hand on Noah's knee. Shrugging one shoulder, he took a deep breath. "Let's listen," he mumbled back.

Sabella fondled an ivory-colored picture frame. Her voice softened. "This beautiful woman is my mother. She died shortly after my birth. She gave me the name I carry, the name inspired by courageous woman—Isabel. I'm sure you don't know it, but it was Isabel who freed the slaves of this great nation. She's revered by the people of my country." A litany delivered with piety.

Now she stepped back, discretely scanning another photo.

"This man, my father, courted Lucifer to give me an education. He gave me food when there was little. He clothed me while he wore rags. He possessed both great strength and overriding weakness. Both qualities resulted in his death."

Pursing her lips, she moved the photo of her father to the far side of the table. Saying nothing, protruding her jaw, she looked about the room as if searching for words.

Perplexed and trapped, Jack and Noah said nothing. Both men felt as though they were being led through a maze, not knowing where they had started nor where they were headed.

"Now," she finally resumed as she reached for the third photo. "This photo, as you can see, is also of a man. A man different from any you have ever met."

Sabella held the picture tight against her shoulder, as if displaying an auction item. It revealed the chiseled features of a most attractive man. Smiling, she exuded wonderment as she then drew the image to her chest.

"This is my João. He was my friend. He was my confidant. But most of all, he was the guardian of my soul, my lover. We were to be married."

But her smile turned into a scowl.

"Men"—she riveted a castigating gaze at Noah and Jack—"like you killed him. Men like you take what is not theirs from this land. My land. João died searching for the truth so that he might stand up against these men." Her eyes were cold. "You may have a story to tell. I have a story too. Although you are guests in my home, I'll tell mine first. You can leave if you wish."

Noah was fidgety again, so Jack quickly took the lead. He had no intention of leaving. Not now. Not yet. She had him entrenched and curious.

"Okay, go ahead," he said sincerely. "We'll listen."

As she walked across the room, her voice became muted. Her comportment slow, deliberate, concise. From all appearances, she was in another place, another time, and alone.

"My grandfather and father achieved great wealth in the time of the rubber barons. Did you know Manaus was once the wealthiest city on this earth? Latex was the lifeblood of my people, my nation. Until Wickham—a thief, a man of your making—stole *Hevea* seeds from the Amazon basin and planted them in other lands."

Now she conveyed her chronicle with contempt, skewing her history to satisfy her narrative.

"And for that, Queen Victoria made him a knight. Men just like you, from North America and Europe, made my people slaves. Railroads were built across the basin to transport men and rubber. For every tie laid, one of my people died. Your famous automaker, Henry Ford, didn't invent the automobile. He simply streamlined labor and became rich. His henchmen rounded up my people and put them in camps. The brothels followed. Our people were cheapened. His city, Fordlandia, was a failure. My people suffered."

Her teeth clenched as she looked at what may just as well have been inanimate shadows of the two men sitting before her.

"You know nothing of my country. You know nothing of its intrinsic life-sustaining beauty or that people call our rain forest 'the lungs of the world.' It will always be vibrant, as long as it is respected. But you are both from a country whose people have pillaged my people—my own family."

Noah shifted in his seat, no longer passively constrained but overtly disapproving.

Jack held out his arm, but he too had reached his breaking point. "Senhorita Sabella," he said, "you're not entirely accurate in your claims. Your wide brush is placing blame and casting aspersions upon Dr. Garrett and me. There's a lot you don't know about us."

"I'll hear you out," Sabella assured them. "But first, you must know more of my family."

In a subtle shift, sorrow replaced lurid acrimony in her voice.

"For a time, they were successful and accomplished. They worked very hard and were blessed with vast holdings along the Rio Negro. But sadly, my family was land rich and money poor. Because they were too trusting, they fell on hard times, their properties slowly dissolving before their eyes. Unknown to my family, the deeds to their land had been fraudulently administered. And my father . . . my beautiful, gullible father . . ." She formed a weary smile. "I never knew that simple, unassuming man harvested lumber far along the most obscure tributaries of the Rio Negro. He was not within the law. His crime was minimal—until he allowed American loggers access to his land."

She delivered these words like a dagger pointing straight at the guests in her home.

"I learned from our priest that my father attended the chapel daily for months prior to his death. My father would weep and beg, Father Silva said. My father begged *not* to be forgiven. He refused confession. Have you ever heard of such a thing?" Her eyes searched the men's. She shook her head. "My father claimed that for some crimes, there could be no forgiveness. Eternal damnation was the only vindication for one such as him. Guilt cries out for punishment, not penance. How is it that one can be so shamed by an indiscretion?"

Again, she searched the faces of the men she had just castigated. For an unintended dimple in time, her eyes locked with Noah's. Magnetized, she remembered the empathy, the compassion he had displayed at that horrific scene the night before.

Noah, stilled now, was unexpectedly drawn into this woman's pain. However, he did not understand the lesson of her father's story—the evisceration caused by irreconcilable self-deception. Being deceived by another can be devastating. Being deceived by one's self can be fatal.

Through the confusion, all Noah understood—or perhaps slowly began to suspect—was that she was trying to justify something. Possibly not only who she was but why.

"His body was found near Mama's gravesite, atop a consecrated hillside nestled among the trees," Sabella continued, more quietly now. "He called that very spot the most important land on the Rio Negro. Lying next to him was an album bearing photographs of my mother and me. I was told there was a note that said, 'Because of men like me, the forest will disappear. *Adeus, verde*'—Goodbye, green. He had committed the cardinal sin. There was a pistol in his hand. A bullet had pierced his brain."

Noah could not control nor disguise his sudden flinch, being seized with the memory of another bullet having pierced another brain. A bullet from Knickknack's gun.

Unaware that Noah was burdened by his own searing memory, Sabella was equally unaware of the irony of her next statements. Leaning forward, stressing her point, she aggressively approached both men with the outstretched fingers of both hands twisted toward herself.

"Bento, my trusted friend, found my father. I gather you call him Knickknack," she said with a sour yet bewildered face, "but Bento has been kind to me, especially since I have lost both Papai and my João—"

Saying that name, Sabella suddenly fell silent. The force of the abrupt stop pushed Noah backward in his seat, as if he'd driven into a wall. He hadn't realized he'd been leaning forward, blatantly bellicose, as she spoke about her Bento, his Knickknack.

Sabella held out the photo frame that Noah and Jack had forgotten she had been clutching to her chest. Once again, she was in another time and place.

"Yes," she said, speaking directly to the photo. "This most handsome man, this most beautiful human being, my betrothed, is João. It is a beautiful name, is it not? He was a brilliant man. It shows in his face. His features are strong, yet his eyes are gentle and kind. Even in this photo, his qualities are revealed. Are they not captivating?"

Noah found it easy to identify with both her love and her grief. Similar words could have come from his own lips, as if in an echo chamber, months ago. But he needed her to push through this pain, to find her way back to her story. And so he was the first to respond.

"Tell me the rest," he urged.

With the inflection only of a whisper, his voice slowly drew Sabella's gaze from the photo. In that moment, she knew the tenor of their relationship had changed. An inextricable connection had become evident. She studied his features this time. His eyes spoke of sorrow—and hunger. She nodded, then continued.

"Bento alone has supported my effort to preserve the land. He may be brash. But he's been the savior of what are now my holdings along this waterway. Without him, I would have lost this land to the bank or to the white loggers my father allowed to pillage our forest. By sifting diamonds from the many tributaries of the main river adjacent to our land, he has satisfied repayment of our debts. Those alluvial diamonds have made Bento a wealthy man."

As if struck by lightning, Noah gasped. *Alluvial*—alluvial diamonds. That was the word neither he nor Jessie could understand that night in the restaurant. The revelation was exciting yet ultimately distressing, as it only posed a greater mystery. Why did a wealthy man with an alluvial diamond source in Brazil try to kill a fat man in a Boston restaurant? It didn't make sense.

Stunned, Noah stared openmouthed and slack-jawed until Jack nudged him. Jack gestured toward the door with one shoulder. It was time leave. They had heard enough.

Following Jack's lead, Noah stood. They each gave a quick bow to their hostess.

"Thank you," Jack said.

Noah nodded, though he didn't know if they were thankful to be leaving or for what they had just heard.

They walked toward the door, then Jack stopped and turned toward Sabella. He dipped his head and slowly caressed one palm against the other, a gesture compatible with wisdom.

"When I first came to Brazil," he softly said, "I was just like my friend here."

He cautiously guided Noah by the back of his neck. Solicitous, he made it clear to Sabella they were on the same page.

"He might be a foreign whitey to you, but he's my friend. As for me, I've learned a lot after living in Manaus for so many years and being married to a native. Sorry to say, Miss Sabella, but you've still got some learnin' to do. This guy knows things you don't."

To Noah, Jack's words were somewhat vindicating.

Noah, hesitant, turned toward Sabella as well. Looking at this woman, he found himself vacillating from disbelief to empathy. Her story was rife with tension from all directions. But would his own tale sound any different?

"You still don't know my story, you know," he said. "Another time?"

She looked at him and nodded. "Let me know when," she answered.

Jack led Noah onto the porch. After the door closed, he took Noah by the shoulders and looked directly into his eyes.

"Listen," he said quietly. "First her father, then her beau? People just don't die like that. Not even around here. And I'm not buying this whole alluvial diamonds story. Yeah, they were a big thing two hundred years ago. And some companies are still finding them in other parts of Brazil. But not on the Rio Negro."

Noah stared blankly at his friend. He was unsure whether this information helped unveil or shroud the mystery.

"There's a connection between you, the girl, her father, João—and yes, even Jessie. We know what—or should I say *who*—that connection is." Escorting Noah down the steps, he placed an arm around his friend's shoulder. "There's a lot to do."

The lingering shadow behind the screen turned and disappeared.

Chapter Eighteen

Acquired knowledge remains fallow before it is tilled with contrived understanding. Yet it is all for naught, lest it be cultivated by wisdom, which is illusive—and for some, innate.

NEITHER MAN SPOKE AS THEY HEADED back toward the Santos. Their fractured thoughts stumbled, trying to find reason through a maze of bits and pieces. Bits and pieces of what—they weren't entirely certain.

Yet.

Driving almost unconsciously, Jack's thoughts ran unchecked. Suddenly, he interrupted the silence with a curt appraisal of what they had just experienced.

"No. Forget the hotel."

As if stricken by a revelation, he snapped his fingers, then veered sharply down a side street. Noah had to brace himself as the van made the hard turn.

"Let's go to the shop instead," Jack said decisively. "We need Flora. She knows all the people at the docks. She'll know about this Knickknack reptile. Besides, she sees things we can't. She can read people by the way they tie their shoes, let alone by the look in their eyes."

The two men returned to silence once again.

Arriving at the shop, Jack led Noah through the back door. Jack knew Flora would be working through the monthly transactions.

"She's no CPA, but she can make a profit from nada," he announced with admiration in his voice as they approached her.

With a welcoming smile, Flora didn't turn toward Jack but rather leaned her head to one side, exposing her neck, giving way for his anticipated kiss.

Noah saw the affection. *That's how it should be.* In that moment, husband and wife were in their own world.

"You two have it all," he said, chin down. His voice was muffled though loud enough to be heard. It was a meager attempt to direct them back into *his* world.

Flora swiveled around, acknowledging Noah's presence. She then looked up at Jack, reached out, and twiddled her fingers over his stomach. "We work at it. But yes, we do have it all."

Jack eagerly pulled up two chairs near Flora. He straddled one as he gestured for Noah to sit in the other.

As if searching, Jack slowly tapped his index fingers to both temples. "Flora, here's the deal," Jack began. "I think I know something but don't have all the pieces."

Flora's eyes narrowed in concentration as Jack methodically recounted everything they knew about Sabella and the man she called Bento. Having heard enough, she minced no words.

"Bento—is that what he calls himself? I've watched him at the diner by the pier, where he regularly has lunch with a ship captain. A German. They work together."

"So, you do know him," Noah said, leaning forward, encouraging her to continue.

"Oh yes." Her voice was discerning and resolute. "That strutting devil is evil. He's a cynic. Controlling and overly confident."

Jack's eyes widened at her unrestrained opinion of a man she hadn't fully met. "I assumed you'd seen this guy around," he said. "But you've never told me any of *this* about him."

She shrugged. "I judge people, just like everyone else. I just don't say anything unless there's a reason. Now, there's a reason."

Once again, Noah was astonished by this woman he initially and obtusely considered to be simple.

Flora looked squarely at Noah. In true character, she read his mind—perhaps his soul.

"Remember, dear Noah, that when we first met, you saw only what you wanted to see. That's because you're like so many others of your kind. But I am different. In order to survive, my people and I have learned to see what *is*. The truth surrounds us. You just haven't learned to see it."

One hand on her hip, Flora continued. "There is a difference between innate learning and formal education. As a young girl, I learned from my people that which can never be put in books. It is passed down through the generations. It's not like hearing, smelling, or seeing. It's more of an extra sense. You don't understand it, just as a person blind from birth will never be taught what it means to see. And then, in addition to this learning"—she pointed both index fingers toward the shelves lined with books—"I also went on to give myself a formal education."

Pointing at a lower tier, she said, "This particular shelf is primary school." Stepping and gesturing to the side, she indicated, "Over here is secondary school." Pointing to a loftier shelf, she added, "And here is the university."

She now stood on her toes, looking directly up at Noah, laughing, with her smile lighting the room. "I'm an Ivy Leaguer."

Finding Flora even more endearing than before, Noah couldn't help but smile, ashamedly blink away a tear, and nod his agreement.

A beaming Jack leaned forward with knees bent and placed both hands on her shoulders. "She certainly is! And when she was in graduate school, I became her pupil."

Without lifting his hands from his wife's shoulders, he turned to Noah. "You see, Dr. Garrett, not all is as it appears. People spend too much time looking for affirmation rather than information. My suggestion is that, starting bright and early tomorrow morning, the three of us start learning more about this guy you call Knickknack. There's more. Gotta be."

At seven the next morning, Flora and Jack picked up a sleepy-eyed Noah in front of the Hotel Santos. Flora, driving, peered through the windshield from beneath the upper arc of the steering wheel. Jack, sitting in the back, adjusted the settings on a long-lensed Nikon.

With singular forethought, Flora took a circuitous route to the wharf, then parked at an inconspicuous, now-decaying portion of the pier. With her wrist draped over the steering wheel, she pointed through the front window.

"That's where we'll find your Knickknack. He's always here early in the morning. He may be a lot of things—thankfully, predictable is one of them."

Jack shook his head and looked at his wife in wonder.

As predicted, the man no one realized was named Caubi was speaking with two stevedores. Still wearing protective leggings, the stevedores had no doubt been forest walking. These were not traditional longshoremen. Their boss handed each a manila envelope, identical to that which Sabella had picked up off the floor at the opera house.

With rapid-fire clicks, Jack's camera captured the moment. Images of jubilant faces with envelopes in hand would add value to Jack's portfolio.

Leaving the VW, Noah, Jack, and Flora casually followed the stevedores as they left the wharf. Passing through a narrow alley littered with last night's garbage, the stevedores walked to the back door of Tito's Diner.

Inherently surreptitious, Flora tucked Jack's camera into her shoulder bag. "You stay here in the alley," she instructed Jack and Noah. Her broad smile transformed into a cantankerously serious frown. "No gringos would ever be seen in Tito's, especially entering though the back door."

This provoked one of Jack's head-bobbing chuckles. Just beginning to experience Flora's whimsical side, Noah realized she was the complete package. In awe, he watched as she made her way into the diner.

The two stevedores had slipped into a corner booth, allowing Flora to enter unnoticed. She lowered herself into a booth. Sitting with her head just above table height, she was stealthy by proportion.

Sharing hits from a common pipe, the stevedores laughed out guttural profanities as they emptied the contents of their envelopes onto the table—packets of American dollars. Beyond tawdry, these men were set apart from the other patrons even more by gnarled faces and open sores dappling their swollen lips.

Flora's camera, its telephoto lens jutting from her purse, captured the provocative scene.

It wasn't long before they were ordered to leave. Satisfied with their reward, they did so without ordering. Brushing past Flora's table, they exuded the smell of burnt plastic. Having been joyous upon entering, they were obnoxiously jubilant now, riding a fresh high.

The photographs would be telling.

Flora returned to the alley, where Jack and Noah stood with their backs tight to a corrugated-metal wall. She eagerly shared what had been captured on camera—the telltale signs of *Erythroxylum*'s grip.

"And your Knickknack pays with greenbacks," she said to Noah. "He must have a connection to the United States." She handed the camera back to her husband. "We're building a revealing portfolio."

Noah stood dumfounded. "Amazing. You do this private eye thing like a pro."

Jack laughed. "Remember her 'education'? Look at the bottom shelf behind the register—Agatha Christie, one end to the other. I'm telling you, this little woman should have been a PI. There ain't nothin' she doesn't know about sleuthin'."

Flora smiled, but she was clearly on to the next step. "Jack and I always go to the plaza before attending the symphony at the Teatro Amazonas," she said. "Your Knickknack is always there too. Always. Sometimes he meets the girl there. In the past, she was accompanied by her boyfriend." She raised her eyebrows, letting her expression say more. "It's Friday, so he'll be there before the performance. We'll be there as well."

She then shook her head disapprovingly at Noah.

"But you, my friend, must first return to your hotel. Your attire isn't appropriate for tonight's performance."

Flora and Jack dropped Noah off at the Santos, with plans to pick him up later that afternoon. The plan was to secure a table for a stakeout at the Praça de São Sebastião.

Stepping into the lobby, Noah expected to find José, the clerk, either sleeping or watching television as was generally the case.

On this occasion, however, José quickly turned and jumped to his feet at the sight of Noah.

"Hello, my dear guest Dr. Garrett. I didn't wish to miss you. You have received a letter. It was left by . . . ah, *uma bela mulher*." He scratched his head. "No, no. What is it in English . . . ?" He tried to find the words. "A beautiful woman? Yes. That is it. Beautiful woman. She insisted I bring it to your immediate attention."

Gripping an envelope in both hands, he handed it to Noah as a formal presentation. Fawning, he continued, "Oh, the writing is lovely, is it not?"

Noah turned the envelope over in his hands, seeing his name on the front. "Yeah. Yes, it is," he curiously muttered more to himself than to the clerk.

Although the letter didn't have a return address, he knew whom it was from. He knew two women in Manaus, and only one was uncommonly beautiful.

"Thanks," he said, turning away slowly. "I'll read it in my room."

Walking up the stairs, he carefully opened the envelope. He stopped at the end of the corridor and gazed at his reflection in the Spanish giltwood mirror. He wondered if the distorted image was a harbinger. If so, just what was in store?

"*C'est la vie*," he finally muttered with a shrug.

Heading into his room, he took a seat on his bed and unfolded the letter on his lap. José was right—the script was lovely. Noah was captivated by it. Calligraphy, no doubt written with great care. Poring over the letter, he was taken by its formal introduction.

Dear Senhor Garrett,

I am truly sorry for my demeanor resulting from our first encounter at the Teatro Amazonas. After your departure from my home, I took time to reflect upon your composure as you became aware of my family's history and circumstance. I sensed your anger when you considered my scathing words. You were incensed by what I said, but to my surprise, you were also sympathetic.

When I first saw you in the Teatro Amazonas, I was upset by what had taken place. I was also angered by who you are. It is easy to tell you are American.

But later, I saw something else as you held the poor child. I saw the empathy you had for the mother. She could have been me. My hair, eyes, and speech are much the same as hers. She and I are, of course, both Brazilian. Yet while you had harshly judged me because of my color, you were sympathetic and caring to another of my kind. I could see compassion in your face, and I could hear it in your voice.

I don't know why you are here, but I know it would be appropriate for us to speak.

Will you meet me tomorrow at the bistro near my home? I will be there at 3:00 p.m. If you decide not to join me, I will understand.

Yours respectfully,

Sabella Almeida

Lost in thought, Noah passed his fingers over the floral onionskin paper. What exactly had she seen in him? For that matter, what had he seen in her?

He placed the letter beneath his pillow, then lay down for a nap. It was an uneasy slumber, with his mind still racing even as he drifted off.

Noah woke with ample time to shower and dress. Before doing so, however, he stood and looked down at the attire he had carefully chosen for the evening and laid out on the bed.

It was enough to nudge a memory. A memory of an evening when he had stood in front of a mirror, practicing his greeting and making every attempt at dressing to please. This was different.

With a corrugated frown, he did a quick shake of his head to rid himself of the memory. "Another life. Another time." This was uttered as a drawn-out, dispirited sigh.

Before heading out the door, he briefly glanced back at his bed. Underneath the pillow, the letter from Sabella remained. He gave its message a quizzical second thought. Coming up with no answers, more muddled than satisfied, he proceeded downstairs and out to the curb, where his friends were waiting.

Jack had reserved a table for three. Ideally located on the periphery of the plaza, the table offered a panoramic view of the opera house as well as the other tables bordering the square. Jack pulled up a chair for Flora as the trio made themselves comfortable and waited for their subject.

Though Flora generally remained true to her heritage by wearing traditional attire, she nevertheless stepped out of form on evenings such as this. When in the plaza, abutting the pristine facade of the Teatro Amazonas, she dressed up for *her man*, a term she frequently used when referring to Jack. Heeled shoes and a pleated smock-style dress were accompanied by a vibrant smile as she clung to Jack's hand.

Jack, not wishing to be revealed in a negative light, wore a white shirt and tie, as was the style, even when temperatures would moisten his brow. He dressed up for Flora.

Punctual as always, the swaggering man they called Knickknack soon arrived, accompanied by his plebeian entourage. With a pointed chin, elevated and defiant, he wore his signature fedora turned up on one side.

How interesting, Noah thought. *That man's attire never changes.* Extending his neck, Noah reached for his own collar and adjusted his ascot.

The trio watched as inconspicuously as possible as Knickknack sat at a table. He leaned back in his chair, raising the front legs from the floor.

Knickknack's lead tagalong—a scruffy sort—did the same but with less success. The trio could see that his teetering attempt and marginal array was inconsistent with flamboyance. Knickknack also seemed aware of the disparity. He shook his head in disgust and appeared to relish his pleb's awkwardness.

Noah watched as his Knickknack folded his hands and twiddled his thumbs as he scanned the *praça*, scrutinizing each table and its occupants. To Noah, the man looked like a seasoned conductor who assessed his audience before each performance.

Then Knickknack's gaze moved toward their table. Noah artfully looked away just in time. Flora and Jack did the same. Noah watched, though, out of the corner of his eye. It did seem as if Knickknack was scrutinizing their table.

"He seems to be taking a special interest in us," Noah said. "It's hard to tell, though."

He spoke these words through a deliberately nonchalant smile so as not to appear suspicious. But then a real smile—albeit a sly one—turned upward.

"Actually, I have an idea. It's called contagious yawning. Silly, but fifty percent of people do it. I'm going to yawn. Watch his table. See what happens."

Noah began with a deep breath, then raised his arms and stretched. Closing his eyes, he produced a gaping mouth and feigned a monstrous yawn. Joe E. Brown would have been proud.

"Well?" he asked as he lowered his arms. "Did you see anything?"

Elbows on the table and forehead in her hands, Flora nodded and suppressed a chuckle. "Yes! Someone yawned. But not Knickknack. It was the scruffy guy next to him. He was definitely watching you."

"I think the whole table is watching us," Jack said with his drink positioned in front of his mouth. "I suppose we do make for an interesting troupe—two gringos and a native woman!"

Nearly convinced but needing one more layer of proof, Noah abruptly jerked his head upward, as though suddenly seeing something in the evening sky. As a reflex, Knickknack and the scruffy guy did the same. Neither knew what they had just telegraphed.

Jack, wishing to extract the most out of this game of tell, turned a questioning look at Flora.

"Well? What do you think? You're the one who can see beyond the obvious."

Happy to oblige, she gave them a small smile. "You and Noah saw a man leaning back on a chair, exuding confidence. But that's only what he wants you to see. Me, I saw a man twiddling his thumbs, though not slowly and deliberately. No. It was fast. Much too fast. Too quick."

She shook her head.

"For me, the picture he makes of himself is inconsistent. For me, he is transparent. Quick means he is concerned. Worried. Why would a confident man be that way? Because he has much on his mind. He is a man hiding from something—or, most likely, with something to hide."

Jack and Noah exchanged glances, thinking of what that might mean for Sabella and her story.

"He may have been watching us, but he doesn't know *we* are watching *him*," Flora continued. "What we know and what he doesn't gives us an advantage. My people know that in order to survive, we must always have the advantage—and we do."

As if to prove her point, Flora nodded toward Knickknack's table, where he and his minions were now looking the other way, scoping out other patrons in the plaza.

Noah openly stared at Knickknack. He thought about the stevedores at the pier, dressed for forest walking, the gnarly men Flora spied from the diner.

"There are no alluvial diamonds," he said quietly, now looking beyond Knickknack's charade.

"Shall we head inside?" Jack suggested, satisfied.

"Yes," Flora replied. As they all rose from the table, she turned to Noah.

"So, you think *your* hands are good for your work as a surgeon? Our featured artist tonight may not be the master himself—Niccolò Paganini, of course—but he does play violin, viola, and guitar. Understand?"

She then looked up at Jack with a furtive, silly smirk and playfully elbowed his ribs. Bantering with levity, they both knew Noah was well out of his league. Attending a world-class symphony performance was their bailiwick, not his.

Noah merely nodded. Preoccupied, he was oblivious to the gentle teasing. For that matter, he remained largely oblivious throughout the entire performance.

The only thing on his mind was that he was to meet Sabella the following day.

Chapter Nineteen

Any subject can be addressed with words. The ultimate truth, however, is always cradled by a single appendage: countenance.

WATCHING SOMEONE IN THE PROCESS of entering a room can be revealing, as it is just that: a process. That which takes place from the time the door opens until the subject is seated can be a story unto itself. As a dynamic event, it must be witnessed from beginning to end.

By intent, Noah arrived at the bistro early, selecting a distant table in an alcove, away from other patrons or prying ears. He neatly arranged a folder in front of him, then waited with eyes fixed on the door.

In time, the door opened, and Noah watched Sabella cross the threshold. She stopped and looked methodically about the room. When she saw him sitting at the far side table, he noticed how her expression wavered between a wince and a smile. Initially, she proceeded slowly, then her gait hastened, exemplifying an evolving confidence.

With conviction, she removed her wide-brimmed hat and tossed her head side to side, allowing ebony hair to unfold across her shoulders. She chose to sit on the far side of the table, no doubt positioning herself at a distance to allow for an easy departure, if that were to become the best option.

From Noah's perspective, she indeed told a story from the moment she entered the room. The least component of that story was that she was timid.

She looked directly at Noah. She cocked her head to one side as she slowly leaned forward with folded hands. She didn't mince words.

"Sir, I presume you to be an intelligent man?" Her inflection made this more of a derisive question than a declarative statement. "I also presume you've had time to take a more critical look at something we seem to have in common. And I believe you may have recognized something in me which I also see in you. My guess is, we share something that came to us long before our lives were shattered."

Curious, he leaned forward. "Okay . . . go on."

"We were groomed to be who we are. *What* we are. I saw you as two different people on the evening we met. One was marred by my preconception," she admitted. "I saw what I wanted to see. As you held the child, though, I had no choice but to see something else—another you. Do you understand me? Am I mistaken?"

Noah replayed what he had just heard. As if contemplating a smile, he nodded. "Yeah. Yeah, I do understand," he finally said. "And . . . you're not mistaken." He took a deep breath. "Who we are and what we become is the product of our experience. There's a difference between doing things right and doing 'em wrong. For me, the difference is rigid—stone rigid. My life's been orchestrated, pounded out on an anvil, driven into me—just like yours."

Noah sat up and leaned forward so far that he was now practically standing. He placed one hand on his chin while the other hand held his elbow close to his body. The posture projected both thought and authority.

"I've heard your story. Now it's my turn. I not only want you to *listen* but, more importantly, I want you to *hear*. You might not like what I'm about to say, but I'm telling you, it's the truth. You might even bet your life on it. Understand?"

With an abbreviated sigh, Sabella leaned back in her chair while crossing her arms as though bracing for a lesson.

His measured diatribe took over an hour to deliver. With controlled indignation, clenched teeth, and poignant fist pounds, his tempered litany was delivered with muscled constraint, considering the setting. Unaltered, he described everything from his modulated childhood to his relationship with Jessie. And through trembling lips, he described an alfresco corner table and a latticed cascade of bougainvillea, literally blood red.

Though initially fixed, Sabella's demeanor began to waver as Noah spoke. She did what all people do when listening to matters of shared substance: she looked inward. She began personalizing everything, from his rigid childhood to his having a well-meaning yet dichotomous parent.

Her varied countenance was clearly dashed, then, when Noah described, in vivid detail, his love and despair as Jessie's eyes remained open, her cheek resting on a checkered cloth.

In conclusion, Noah looked directly at Sabella and placed both hands on the table. "And that brings us to the here and now. When I arrived in this green hell, I found the person I was looking for. I knew him by the way he dressed, the way he walked, and even the way he wore his cockamamy hat. That bastard who murdered my Jessie is the same man you call your friend, your guardian angel. I call him Knickknack. You call him Bento."

Sabella was stunned, breathless. "You—you must be mistaken."

He put his face directly in front of hers. Slamming his fist on the table with rigorous constraint, he snarled yet remained blisteringly emphatic. "I'm not!"

Startled, a few patrons glanced over. Something about the scene at the far table was too much to bear, though. They quickly looked away.

"I have been following him with Jack and his wife, Flora." Noah looked about the room and continued, lowering his voice. "We know just about everything. We know what he's doing. And we know where he's doing it."

Unbelieving and motionless, Sabella murmured, "No. It just can't be. Bento's an unusual man, yes. At times shamefully rude, I'll admit. But he's always been kind to my family . . ."

Noah slapped open the folder in front of him, revealing the photographs Jack and Flora had taken the day before on their reconnaissance mission. He indelicately pushed them in front of her.

"Look at these," he said. "See his cronies with envelopes filled with money? Look familiar? Those envelopes are identical to the one in your purse the night I ran into you. Yes, I saw you try to hide it," he said in response to her shocked look. "And actually, the reason I ran into you that night was because I had my eyes only on him—your friend Bento."

"This can't be," she said, gesturing to the photos with a trembling hand. "It simply can't."

He drove a lancinating stare at Sabella and pointed his finger in her face. "What I don't understand is why the hell you're part of it. A woman like you seems an unlikely accomplice. Why are you doing it?"

Shaken, she lowered her head for a moment, then raised it and looked directly at Noah once again.

"I'm not what you think I am. I've done nothing wrong. He gives me money, yes. I give him preferred tickets to the opera. And we make—I mean, *I* make his rent reasonable. Nothing more. He's . . . very good to me," she said tentatively.

"I bet he is!" Clearly agitated, Noah sent a message by scanning Sabella from head to toe. "Are you blind? He certainly isn't. Look at you!" He reached out and placed his hand beneath her chin. "Are you sure there are no *favors* in exchange for that envelope of cash?"

She batted his hand away. "Stop it!"

With a brief glance down at herself, she wrapped her arms over her chest. It was an instinctive defense even while her eyes went on attack.

"How *dare* you? I don't do anything improper! That money is part of a *business arrangement*." Her words were clipped. "Bento works very hard for the diamonds he retrieves from the estuary adjacent to my land. That money I receive in exchange is just enough to pay off most of my debts and allow me to retain the land. The land, by the way, that was nearly stolen by the banks." Emboldened by the comfortable rhetoric, she now pointed a finger at Noah. "The land *your* people came here to plunder and steal."

Noah opened his mouth to protest, but Sabella steamrolled past him.

"What's left of that money allows me to attend the university, where I study to preserve that which is rightfully *ours*. My studies are not just for me but for all of Brazil and her people. My parents' greatest wish was for me to be educated. And my father *killed* himself out of shame for having sold lumber illegally in order to fulfill these dreams for me."

"Oh my God," Noah groaned, throwing his hands up. His eyes were wild. "You're being duped. He's using you! I know it! And unless you're a fool, you know it too. The money doesn't come from diamonds. There are no diamonds!"

Agitated, he turned from the table, placing both hands to his temples in disgust. "She doesn't know," he mumbled to himself. "She honestly doesn't know!"

"Doesn't know what?" Sabella demanded.

Noah squeezed his hands against his head, then released. His hands remained suspended in the air, inches away from his temples, while he drew five long breaths. Then he slowly lowered his arms, pushed back his chair, and stood. She watched in confusion as he came around the table and sat by her side. Placing a consoling hand on her shoulder, his tone softened.

"Listen to me, Sabella."

Something in her shifted, hearing him use her name.

"The money comes from the sale of something more valuable than diamonds," Noah said slowly, carefully. "It comes from a drug. Cocaine. You may not realize it, but you're in the business of growing cocaine. It's almost certainly growing on your land. He's sending it out of the country with the help of a German ship captain. You've seen him. I know you have. Right?"

Clearly choking back a verbal response, she slowly furrowed a questioning brow. After a moment, with her head moving side to side slowly, she acknowledged her own disbelief. "Yes. Yes, I've seen him," she said.

Noah paused, preparing himself to say the hardest piece of all. "And your father and your João . . . ? I fear they didn't die in the way you've been led to believe. I believe Knickknack—Bento—killed them. Like he killed my Jessie."

It may have taken only a brief moment or an eternity, but Sabella's expression evolved along with her understanding. Her appearance began as a barren mask, which, as a man of medicine, Noah could recognize as clearly as he could the facies of Parkinson's. Then her brow knitted, puzzled. At last, her face sagged from the weight of shame. She covered it with her protective, accepting hands.

"Yes," she said, a revelation which came as a whisper. It was followed by a discerning nod.

Each was now transformed.

"You must listen." Noah's delivery was measured, delicate, and decisive. "Here's what we're gonna do: Don't let him know we've spoken. He's keeping an eye on Jack, Flora, and me, but he doesn't know we've been keeping an eye on him. That gives us the advantage. As for you, don't let on a thing. Meet him and collect the money as if nothing has changed. Thank him profusely, if that's what you've done in the past. Got it?"

With wide eyes, she nodded.

"When he meets the ship captain, he spends the entire day in the city. That's when Jack and I will go to your land—with your permission," he quickly added.

Again, she nodded, this time with more resolve.

"Flora's people have already promised to bring us there by a route he and his men can't find," he said. "Her people know more about the river than any of us—or even any of you."

He almost smiled, thinking about the insights Flora might have to offer about urbanized Brazilians such as Sabella as compared to her own indigenous kind.

"We'll leave before dawn tomorrow," Noah continued. "Remember, you must meet him just as you always have. Take the money, act normal, and don't say anything about our meetings. Understand?"

"This is almost unbelievable . . . but I'll do it," Sabella agreed. She placed her hands in his. "I'm not entirely sure why, but I do believe you." There was a long pause. "Strange . . . You lost the one you love, and I lost not one but two."

A small wave built inside Noah as he contemplated the losses, the pain. He waited for it to crest before he spoke.

"Yes, but it's not so strange anymore. Now we know it leads to one man. The man who still needs you. For now, that need is keeping you safe."

Sabella slowly rose from the table as if wrapped in an impassive void. She placed a pensive hand on Noah's cheek. "I'll be at the Teatro Amazonas tomorrow as usual. Make your plans."

They were now two different people.

Chapter Twenty

Individual pieces of a puzzle, perceived as probing remnants, may coalesce to create an ominous portrait—racked with pain.

AFTER A SHORT, RESTLESS NIGHT, JACK—accompanied by two of Flora's short and very dark-skinned cousins—met Noah in front of the Santos before dawn. Each wore leggings.

"Here," Jack said, handing Noah a similar pair. "Protection. You'll need it. We'll be forest walking. It'll still be dark when we get there, so you better put 'em on now."

The river was flat as the four men motored their way through the waters of the Rio Negro. Breaking the silence, the reverberating, shearing echo of howler monkeys could be heard for miles along the river.

"Kind of an eerie sound," Noah said, awkwardly hunkered at the center of the boat. "Loons are sort of that way, but their sound is more forlorn, not quite so macabre.

Maybe haunting?" All the while, he tried to erase from his mind that even these sounds could prove prophetic.

Paulo, a man no taller than the outboard motor, smiled as he managed the helm. The night sky defining the undulating tree line was all he needed to navigate past the islands.

Durante, leaning over the bow, watched for deadheads—submerged logs. They were prevalent byproducts of the illicit pilfering of lumber.

The tranquilizing drone of the motor established a soothing atmosphere for whispered conversation. Both Jack and Noah realized that small talk goes a long way when trying to ward off fear. Neither knew what to expect, whom they might meet, nor how many there might be.

After nearly an hour, Paulo suddenly veered starboard, slipping through an outcropping tangle of trees. The maneuver caused Jack and Noah to grasp the gunwales for fear of being swept off or capsizing. Both of their escorts, being in their element, made less than furtive attempts to conceal their fanciful smiles.

For Jack and Noah, it appeared they were running aground. There was just enough light from the waning gibbous moon to see when they had to bob, weave, and duck beneath low-hanging branches. Noah raised an accepting brow and breathed a sigh of relief when they eventually found themselves on open water once more.

It was a brief return, however. Moments later, they suddenly swerved again, sliding between yet another assemblage of overhanging branches. The serpentine estuary undulated between trees on either side of the boat.

As they moved farther and farther away from the main river, Jack and Noah once again resorted to small talk to help exorcise their anxiety. It did no such thing, as their entire exchange was noticeably tainted by uneasy glances. How on God's earth did these two guys have any clue as to where they were? Flora's cousins were all that existed between Jack and Noah being forever lost and arriving at their destination.

"One hour," said Paulo with quiet confidence, no doubt sensing the anxiety. He and Durante shared a calm that eased the concerns of their passengers.

Far into the backwater—exactly one hour later—Paulo turned off the motor. Using long poles, he and Durante eased the boat toward land. The sky was now dark blue, with waning stars preceding the dawn.

"Very close," came as a barely audible whisper from Durante. "We begin forest walking soon. We must be quiet."

Like Paulo, he had little to say but clearly knew what to say and when to say it.

Once all four men had stepped onto dry land, Paulo and Durante pulled the boat beneath low-hanging branches. They signaled Noah and Jack to follow as they pressed catlike into the forest. Both Paulo and Durante carried machetes but used them sparingly, keeping noise to a minimum.

Noah was surprised that walking came with ease. Little direct sunlight reached the forest floor, so vegetation was sparse, but an intertwining root system both beneath and through the trees gave support to what appeared to be a never-ending canopy.

"No touch," one of the cousins warned without looking back. The command was purposefully hushed. Neither

Noah nor Jack could detect whose it was. "Don't reach for branches or even grass. It can be very sharp."

Regardless of who had issued the warning, Noah and Jack knew to take heed.

For the next thirty minutes, not a word was spoken. Just when Noah began to wonder what ancient wisdom allowed these men to traverse such labyrinths on both land and water, Paulo, in the lead, turned and placed a finger to his lips. He then pointed to his ear. He could hear something.

Moving forward, each now on hands and knees, the men came across razor wire flanking a small clearing that housed a rectangular building. Its roof, covered with sticks and leaves, resembled the forest floor—no doubt to camouflage it from being spotted from the air. Several men stood near what appeared to be a firepit.

"Manioc," whispered Paulo, who shook his head with a condescending smile.

Manioc, being the ultimate staple for all indigenous Brazilians, traditionally occupied the table at nearly every meal. Apparently even when brewing coca.

Although visibility was limited, Jack and Noah recognized two of the men near the fire. They were the same men Flora had photographed at Tito's Diner. Their crackling voices carried well through the morning air. It was obvious they and the other men were preparing to leave.

Finally, they exited through a metal gate, each carrying a sack over his shoulder. After securing a chain, they made their way along a narrow yet well-traveled path to the river. When the men were out of earshot, Paulo turned to Jack and Noah.

"That path leads to a tributary about a mile away," he mouthed in near silence.

Paulo then slipped beneath the wire and crawled ahead. Creeping past what appeared to be a bamboo pen, he carefully peered through a side window of the building. After a moment, he signaled the others to join him.

"No one here," he said, now with only a bit more volume. "We're alone. But from what I can see inside, they'll return."

Noah opened the door, peering inside what was no doubt a workstation. As expected, it housed provisions for processing cocaine. As Noah walked through the building, an offensive chemical odor of burnt plastic or rubber made him cringe. Drying machines, barrels of kerosene, sulfuric acid, carbonate salt, and lime cluttered the room. Particulate fragments of cocaine had been carelessly strewn on the floor. The detritus was evidence that the product was being prepared in two forms: as freebase, which those doing the cooking could smoke for its immediate effects; and as powder for packaging and world distribution.

Closing the door quietly, Noah walked the perimeter of the building. Although climate conditions in the forest weren't always ideal for coca, a large overlying canopy shaded the planting area. It created a cooling effect, optimizing germination and plant growth.

"Quite the operation," Noah said, taken aback. Bearing a quizzical frown, he puckered his lips and bit down on the inside of his cheeks before looking at Jack. "Now what?"

"Proof. We get proof." With confidence and purpose, Jack pulled his camera out of his backpack.

He had barely lifted the viewfinder to his eye when Paulo called out.

"Noah, Jack—come."

Paulo stood by Durante, who was now on his knees in the bamboo pen. Durante passed his fingers along the bars. After rubbing them together, he brought them to his nose.

"Blood. Old, dry blood. And here"—he plucked something from the dirt floor—"a spent shell casing."

Noah peered into the pen. "Probably goats. They gotta eat."

"No," Durante said with the eye of wisdom. He shook his head slowly. "This pen isn't for goats."

Durante picked up what appeared to be a tattered braided band. Noah tried to remember where he'd seen something like that before.

"No, this isn't a pen at all," Durante now said. "It's a cage . . . but not for animals."

The camera clicked incessantly as Jack took pictures of everything—the building, the planting area, the cage. When he lowered the camera, the others could finally see his dumbfounded expression.

"Oh my God," Jack said, running his palm down his face and mouth. "We hafta leave this place just like we found it. Leave the braid and the casing. The pictures say it all."

The men left as they had entered. Once on the other side of the razor wire, Noah looked back at the cage. The sun passing through the bamboo bars cast linear shadows across the ground. Shaking his head in disbelief, he thought of the casing, the braided band . . . the blood.

Chapter Twenty-One

Transference—a binary process that needs never to be spoken. In both directions, it carries the same message.

LATER THAT AFTERNOON, A BLISTERING SUN reflected off the Teatro Amazonas as a conflicted Noah Garrett stood pensively beneath its majestic entry portico. The day before, he'd asked Sabella's permission to search for the convincing truth that might exist on her land. Now he wondered how he should deliver his message.

He watched from afar as she made her ascent along the promenade leading to the front entry of the grand opera house. Having unwittingly shed the manacles of prejudice, he looked at this woman with a sense of caring for the first time. Her gait fluid, she cast a striking figure—lustrous black hair wisped by a refreshing morning breeze.

So beautiful. So sad.

She was right, he realized. They had both shared a burden that had existed long before they each experienced personal loss.

What she might be thinking at that very moment was difficult for Noah to know. Any peace she had would soon be shattered. Learning that João had been brutally murdered by the very man with whom she had entrusted the welfare of all she held sacred—it might prove too much to bear.

Looking upward, he searched the sky for solace. With a raised brow and a quick resolute shake of his head, he managed a deep sigh. *Strange*, he thought. Not wishing her pain, his unintended transition now left him struggling with anguish.

Nearing the top step, Sabella noticed Noah leaning against the entry. Not having witnessed his distress, she thought he looked handsome in that setting, framed by the arch. She smiled, then immediately wondered why.

She quickly reconfigured her bearing to one of rightful concern. She had been unsure whether he would come tonight. She was simultaneously pleased and distressed that he had.

Unsure how to begin, Noah acknowledged her arrival with a subtle, forcibly reluctant wave.

She stopped directly in front of him. "I know you have information for me. But first, I have information for you. Bento left Manaus with his captain friend a little while ago. He'll likely be gone for at least ten days. On these trips, he leaves on the *Fuga* but returns by air. The final destination of the ship is always Boston."

A quick moment of pause settled between them. They were both thinking of a particular evening in Boston, an evening that brought their worlds together.

"By now," she continued, "I hope you understand I'm not a weak woman. I also hope you understand that one can become resolute, strengthened, with certain experiences." She paused, letting the silence yet again speak for both of their stories. "So, Dr. Garrett, just what is it you have for me?"

With her chin up and a look of restrained trepidation, she held out both hands with palms up—she was ready to receive.

Noah felt braced and relieved by her candor. His words, this truth, would not break her. Although she would internalize this new grief, she would do so with decorum and acceptance. Noah saw this woman with brown eyes and dark skin as a cultivated image of himself. Both were hewed by circumstance, all the while honed and nurtured a world apart.

Mustering a cautionary look, Noah pulled a folder from beneath his arm. "I have some information. It's something . . . something you have to see."

She nodded and accompanied him onto the adjoining praça. They sat at opposite ends of a bench. A gentle breeze rustled the leaves, conveying a calming distraction.

Although neither addressed it, they each detected the nearly imperceptible transformation in the way they related to each other. It was a telling mutation for two people whose initial encounter was more of a confrontation than an introduction.

Noah searched for the right words. Finally, he placed the folder between them, opened it, then arranged the photos Jack had taken the previous day.

Sabella picked them up one at a time, perusing each thoroughly before setting all but one back on the bench.

"I know what this is," she said, gazing at the photo of the braided band from the fishing cap. With genteel acquiescence, she added, "Where did you find it?"

"Jes—"

Immediately crimson, Noah froze before uttering another sound. How—why—did he nearly call her Jessie?

Sabella recognized his gaffe. "It's okay—one of those Freudian things," she said softly. "Don't be embarrassed. We all do it."

"I guess so . . . ," he said, sounding unconvinced.

Fleetingly silenced by his own epiphany, Noah realized he hadn't interchanged names so much as superimposed feelings. Shaking his head, he looked back to the photos, more determined than ever to let the truth come forward.

"*Sabella*"—it was a careful enunciation—"these are from your property off the Rio Negro. I can prove what's happening there and who's doing it. It's your Bento. He's growing coca and manufacturing cocaine on your property."

Her eyes were locked on the photo still in her hands; she wouldn't look up at him.

Noah slowed his words now. "João didn't die falling from his boat. He died in a bamboo cage next to the building where the cocaine is being produced. I also found a shell casing on the ground beside the cage."

Although reticent, Noah directed his gaze directly at Sabella. Her head was still down. He began to raise his hand, wishing to reach out and gently lift her chin. But then he stopped. He sensed that she needed to experience this moment in her own time, in her own power. So instead, he spoke.

"I'm sorry."

The words would have seemed trite had they not been spoken by someone who so deeply recognized her pain.

Tears running down her cheeks, Sabella glanced through the photos on the bench once again, reaching down to lightly touch each one. Then she returned to the photo in her lap, slowly rubbing her finger over its shiny surface.

"I bought that hat for João. I bought it for him because he loved Greek history, especially mythology. We talked of going to Greece with our children one day, when they were grown." She was sobbing now. "We had already named them—Apollo for a boy and Athena for a girl. Not even Portuguese. Just a Greek god and goddess."

She managed a chuckle as she sniffed and wiped her eyes.

"João and I played childish games. We shared myths and fantasies. Who would do such a silly thing?" She laughed through a torrent of tears, then looked up at Noah with a quick shake of her head. "You wouldn't understand." It was as deflective as it was self-deprecating.

A single tear dropped onto the photo. Defiantly, she gave it a hard blot with her thumb.

Noah reflected upon this narrative of two people—two people in love, with the anticipation of all that was to be.

He knew two other lovers who had shared childish games and fantasies.

Dreams. Just dreams, he thought.

His hand began to rise again. This time, he didn't stop. He reached over, taking both of her hands in his. "But I do understand—completely. Jessie and I were like you and João. We joked and teased a lot. And just like you and João, we spoke of what we would name our children."

A small smile crept across Sabella's face. She leaned forward. "Please go on," she urged.

In that moment, Noah felt an effervescence, a lightness, rising to the surface. His words poured out.

"Well, my favorite author is Thomas Hardy. *Jude the Obscure, The Return of the Native*—great. You would probably like *Tess of the d'Urbervilles*—pathos wearing a cloak of naivete from cover to cover. Just like you, me, and everyone else."

Unconsciously, he had let go of her hands in order to make enthusiastic and animated gestures. Her smile grew with each jubilant swirl of his hands.

"Anyway," he continued, "Jessie and I decided to name our first son Thomas, after Thomas Hardy. I especially like the way it's pronounced by Europeans, with the emphasis on the last syllable—*moss*. You know? 'Toe-moss'?"

They laughed together.

"And we played silly little games too," he said, eager to share more. "Sometimes we'd make up wild stories about people we'd see on our walks in Boston Common. We'd pretend they were spies or criminals or—heaven forbid—*foreigners*."

With chagrin, he covered his face with his hands. He and Sabella both recognized the abundance of cultural barriers and prejudices they were shattering. Any previous discord hadn't come from a superficial abrasion but from an indelible stain nesting deep inside.

His first impression of her had been triggered by an unlucky incident, the color of her skin, and the latitude at which she lived. She, at that same moment, saw a foreigner who just happened to be white. Most Brazilians saw the label *gringo* as a benign appellation meaning "foreigner." But Sabella's personal lexicon had been honed by a vivid anthology of rubber barons, pilfering loggers, and grotesque butchers.

They had shared that experience and had learned from it, and now it was gone. Once angry, tattered remnants from the same cloth, they had both changed.

He peeked through his fingers and winked at her.

Laughing, her smile now spread over her eyes and whole face.

Noah mirrored her, smiling as he hadn't done since that grisly evening. He was no longer living his pain; he was sharing his happiness. This transformation had begun that day in the bric-a-brac shop, when he had emptied his soul to a diminutive woman who knew so much more about life than he. Flora was right: *becoming* whole and *being* whole are two separate things.

"Funny, isn't it?" he said, softly now. "I can talk about this with you. I can share a part of . . . well, you know."

"Yes, I do know." Her tone was the essence of kindness as she looked not toward Noah but directly into his eyes. "You're a real person. I like you this way. I love your excitement. I look at you and see myself—who I am and can be beyond all this." She nodded to the photos still between them.

Reaching forward, over the photos, he placed his hands on her cheeks. "Sabella, we can't go back to where we were—I mean, where we were before we first met. Something's changed."

"Yes—us," Sabella said, now eye to eye. She embraced him with a slowly evolving tranquil smile. "We've changed. We're alive again."

They lingered like this for a moment. By degrees, their lives were beginning to coalesce. Noah could tangibly feel it—a bonding energy between them.

Then Sabella pulled back and clapped her hands together as an epiphany. "I have an idea. I hope I'm not misreading . . . us, but I'd like to bring you to a special place, one that means a lot to me. A place where one might make new memories rather than live with the old ones."

Noah nodded, clinging to her every word. The "us" part was especially satisfying.

"I'd like you to see the meeting of the waters, where the Solimões and Rio Negro are reluctant to join," she said. "The ferry could bring us to a village with a single quaint restaurant. We can leave tomorrow morning—the excursion landing, six thirty?"

She rustled in her purse for pen and paper, jotted down the address, then handed it to him, her fingers lightly touching his.

Noah nodded with a tempered grin. "Six thirty tomorrow. That's just fine."

With that, she gathered her purse, vigorously grasped his hands one more time, then headed back to the theater.

Although not perceived at a conscious level, their parting was a separation that served only as figurative distance. Noah, now with dutiful observance, stood attentive and watched Sabella accordingly blend into the majesty of the Teatro Amazonas—beauty upon beauty.

Their roles could have been reversed, yet their mindsets would have been the same.

Returning to the Santos, questioning what had transpired, he relived the events of the day. He couldn't help but feel he had established a sense of belonging in this new world. And a weight seemed to have been lifted from his shoulders, though he wasn't entirely sure why.

One thing was certain: he had developed a deep affection for this woman.

As Noah entered the Santos, he adopted a sense of reverence as he found José slouched in his chair, chin to his chest, sleeping comfortably at his post behind the front desk. Out of courtesy, Noah tiptoed past the man and up the stairs.

But even with Noah's stealth, José heard him enter. The roused manager rose to his feet and scurried along the corridor to Noah's room, trying not to be intrusive. Head down with his eyes peering upward, he clasped his hands to his abdomen as he spoke in a whisper.

"Dr. Garrett, pardon, may I interrupt you? There was a man here earlier this afternoon. He inquired about any americanos who might be staying at our lovely hotel. As no other americanos have stayed here since the Ford man, I knew he must be inquiring about you. He said he was a survey man." José raised an eyebrow. "I might be old, but I'm no fool. I said nothing. He left, but not before looking at the registration book."

Noah nodded, curtailing a gritty smile. His response was delivered with calm. "Thank you. I'm sure there's no problem."

So, Knickknack, too, was looking—though he still didn't know why. It would appear that the game of cat and mouse was being played on Noah's terms.

Expectations may be nothing more than a morass of open-ended wishful thinking.

Perhaps, with the right ingredients, dreams can come true.

EARLY THE NEXT MORNING, Noah walked to the pier with newfound, unyielding anticipation. The marketplace adjacent to the boat landing was abuzz with merchants, buyers, and sellers, each with an agenda. They were all unaware of his allayed expression enhanced by a smile.

These people had changed since he first arrived in Manaus a lifetime ago. They were no longer looking *at* him nor were they defined by brown or black. They had become just people, some with purpose, others simply milling.

"I have our tickets," came a friendly greeting from the bow of the *Ibis*. "Come aboard."

Looking up, Noah could see Sabella leaning over the front rail.

Meeting her atop the gangway, Noah suddenly forgot to breathe. She was in a black sleeveless dress that set her apart from others on the pier. And she stood taller than expected thanks to open-toed pumps. She was the picture of smart and casual, elegance and beauty—a side of her he had not seen before.

"You look . . . different," he managed, once he was able to reengage a fumbling tongue. He clenched his jaw, jutted his chin, and capped it all with a laborious swallow. "You're . . . taller. I haven't seen you like . . . you are now. Don't get me wrong," he quickly stammered. "You look . . . wonderful."

"Thank you." She looked down at herself, then back up at Noah. "I wanted to dress more like someone, mm, possibly from North America? As one might dress in, say, Boston?" With an alluring smile brushed with a raised brow, she held both hands to her cheeks. "Oh, I'm embarrassing myself!"

"Hardly," Noah replied. Glancing down at his own attire, he blushed. "I mean, I'm wearing the same clothes I did yesterday. I'm the one who should be embarrassed!"

At ease and yet fearfully out of bounds, he stepped forward, placed his hands on her shoulders, and kissed her on the cheek.

"Thank you," she said again.

She stared at him for just a moment, then leaned forward and kissed him on the lips.

"Soft. Your lips are soft," she whispered before pulling away with a choreographed come-hither wave. "They serve breakfast on the ferry. I know the captain. He'll treat us well."

Indicating they'd like a table, Sabella motioned to a crewman, who also served as a diligent gopher. As they waited, she and Noah stood face-to-face along the Brazilian cherry rail. Silence settled between them, as did subtle unease. Their first moments together had been affectionate and unrestrained, but now they found themselves both in and, for Noah, surrounded by untested waters. They had not yet settled into their new surroundings nor their new dynamic.

Sabella protruded the tip of her tongue, as if nurturing a thought. She slowly passed it along her upper lip as she fawningly ran her fingers along the rail.

"Beautiful, isn't it? It's very hard—the rail, that is. You can see that it carries a lustrous sheen, as do many of the hardwoods of my nation."

"Yes," Noah said, running his hand along it too. "It is beautiful." He looked up at her and smiled.

A calm washed over them both. Small talk, by design, had a sensuous and comforting affect that served to establish a welcoming mood. Remaining in her element, Sabella felt free to assume command by respectfully extracting a menu from a passing waiter.

"We should eat light. We call this *café da manhã*." She pointed at a photo on the menu. "It literally translates to 'morning coffee,' but it also just means 'breakfast.' Bread is important too. There's *pão francês*. Sort of a French roll.

For me, I like cheese bread best—*pão de queijo*. And this"—teasingly, she pointed to another photo—"we call *suco de laranja*. You call it orange juice."

Noah could only laugh at her banter, which couldn't have been more reassuring.

"Don't worry—I'll order," she said as she tweaked his chin.

It reminded him of another time. Another place. Only now, the pain was gone.

Minutes later, Noah and Sabella were seated at a portside window. They watched as the dock lines were cast. Like the ferry, Sabella and Noah were no longer tethered—in their case, tethered to prying eyes and innuendo emanating from the city.

The black swirls of the Rio Negro reminded Noah of the first time he had traveled these waters with Paulo and Durante. What had seemed ominous then was tranquil now. This was different. The muffled *putt-putt* of the diesel engines was soothing. A sense of peace was restored.

A crew member with a camera strapped around his neck hurriedly breezed past them. He stopped abruptly, however, when he caught a glimpse of the striking woman in the black dress. He approached their table politely but eagerly.

"Senhorita, may I?" he asked her, lifting the camera partially to his eye.

Blushing, Sabella nodded. She composed herself, gazing into the camera with bright eyes and a beautiful smile.

The photographer gave Sabella an approving look. "Your photo will be ready upon your departure. A gift from the captain." He winked at Noah. "A gift for *you*, perhaps!"

Once again, Sabella blushed.

After breakfast, they returned to the bow. With her back to the rail, Sabella smiled as Noah mouthed a "wow" while looking down the river, its expanse greater than he could have ever imagined.

"Jack was right," he said. "This *is* the big one."

Sabella turned now to watch the water. With her shoulders back and her hands on the rail, she was an alluring sight. A figure composed.

"Impressive, isn't it?" she said. "I think about it—the river, that is—a lot. Her true origin, though questioned by some, makes her longer than her African counterpart, the Nile. For me, it's easy. This is the most magnificent river on the planet." She drew a deep breath. "I don't recall where I read it, but someone once said, 'Life, for the river Amazon, tranquil from its inception, evolves from unadorned droplets of rain, tractable snows, and Andean mountain mists, only to shed its halcyon ways to become a quisling renegade to those who unassumingly intrude.'"

She let the words steep in Noah's mind for a moment, then tilted her chin and shoulder coquettishly.

"Sort of poetic, isn't it? I like it—the flow and rhythm of the words. Like it should be put to music."

Noah looked out at the water and nodded. "The flow—yes."

"Embraced by a one-hundred-million-year-old rain forest, this river holds mystery, sustains life, and concedes death without remorse," Sabella continued, the poetry and passion her own now. "If the earth suddenly lost this rain forest and its water, life would eventually end—not just here but everywhere. So, even for those who reside at different latitudes"—she pointed at Noah—"it's still the essence of their very existence. Like us, this river and its forest are not immortal. The river is alive, and all living things can die."

As if in a trance, she scanned the water and its distant shores. She held her clenched fists together, pressed tightly to her mouth.

"They say that Egypt is the gift of the Nile. If that is the case, then this very planet—this earth, your earth, my earth, its every breath—is the gift of the Amazon and her magnificent rain forest. Just thinking of her gives me strength and courage." She now grasped Noah's shirt, pulling him next to her. "Wouldn't you agree?" With a touch of the whimsical, her delivery was both artful and reverent.

"You love your river, and you love your land," Noah told her. "You're a steward of both. I respect you for that. But mostly, I respect you for who you are." As if caressing a delicate flower, he passed his fingers gently over her face and lips. "You're quite the teacher . . . and you're very beautiful."

He paused as her face flushed with delight, then he took his turn at poetry.

"Loving requires understanding, respect, and, most of all, introspection. Love is a personal thing. Its holder may accept it as though it came from another place. But it doesn't. It's self-created. It comes from within. Loving doesn't tell only of that which is loved—it defines the lover."

Holding his hand, she kissed his palm. Slowly looking up, she asked, "Where did that come from?"

"It came from me. It came from *you*," he added. "You brought it out of me. Your beauty is in your words, your passion, and it comes from a very special place. It's yours to share, and I thank God you're sharing it with me."

And with that, Noah stepped back. As if directed by wisdom from afar, he looked celestially into her eyes. Initially saying nothing, he slowly reached forward and caressed her face. With tears streaming down his cheeks, he looked up and whispered, "Thank you."

A cooling breeze awarded the hot and sultry Amazon basin a brief reprieve as the *Ibis* distanced herself from Manaus. Sabella and Noah, looking over the starboard rail, were soon witnesses to an iconic yet peculiar sight: the meeting of the waters.

Here, the brown of the Solimões and the black of the Rio Negro came together and touched—but only touched. By their very nature, they were immiscible. The distinction was vivid. Downriver, the waters would, by circumstance, coalesce into one by cataracts, angry swirls, and violent eddies.

Neither Sabella nor Noah spoke as the ferry straddled the demarcation. Instead, they gazed at each other, sharing meaning in silence. At one time similarly immiscible, they too had been brought together by tumultuous forces.

Chapter Twenty-Three

As Diotima of Mantinea understood, love comes in stages. The first defined by something we don't have—aroused by the sight of individual beauty.

AFTER SEVERAL HOURS, THE FERRY DOCKED at a small jetty. Sabella and Noah disembarked, as did other passengers. As they all shuffled down the pier, a voice called out from behind.

"Senhorita!"

Everyone looked back to see the photographer making his way through the group to Sabella. His arm was raised high above his head as he made his way through the line of people.

"Senhorita, your photo," he said, catching up to Sabella and Noah. He lowered his arm, presenting an envelope.

Immediately wide-eyed, Sabella accepted the envelope and pressed it to her chest. She stepped away from Noah and dipped her chin as a shield, lest the contents of the envelope did not meet with her satisfaction. She held her breath and slowly drew the photo from the envelope. After an elated burst of satisfaction, she finally presented it with outstretched arms to Noah.

"For you. A keepsake. My gift. From me to you!"

Noah first looked at the photo and then at Sabella. The photo had indeed captured her spirit, her vitality, her essence.

"It's beautiful. You're beautiful," he said. He smiled and pressed the photo to his lips. "Thank you."

From the pier, Sabella and Noah could see the entire village and its only street at a glance. Along the cobbled walk was one restaurant, one shop, a grocery store, a small inn, and a church with weathered white paint. On the shore was the shell of a boat under construction. This quaint village—with its passion flowers, anthurium, monkey brush, but no prying eyes—met with their approval.

Scampering, inquisitive children skipped alongside the pier with their hands out, tugging on Sabella's dress and Noah's pant legs as they left the landing.

"*Dinheiro para doces?*" they asked—Money for candy?

With smiling faces, they knew their begging wasn't frowned upon. It was a scene quite different from the streets of Rio de Janeiro, where the art of begging was carried out by pleas, sunken faces, and bona fide anguish.

Sabella and Noah moved along with a group of eager passengers heading toward the store. Intrigued, Noah made to follow but was stopped when Sabella tugged on his arm.

"They're buying *chicha*. It's a fermented drink made from manioc root," she explained, shuddering. "But the local women 'process' it in their mouths before it gets to yours!"

Noah was relieved he had not only a tour guide but a protector as well.

"I want to take you where my father took me as a child," Sabella said, nodding toward the edge of town, where the transition from village to forest was abrupt. "He knew the forest, its critters and creatures. For all his shortcomings, he was an excellent teacher."

"I'm sure he was, just like you," Noah added graciously, taking her hand. "I would love to explore the forest with you."

Standing before the storefront window, they looked at their reflections, one clad in an elegant black dress and the other in a wrinkled encore. The sight made Sabella laugh.

"Perhaps we should head inside to do some shopping. Neither of us is dressed for the climate nor the forest. For sure, this dress won't last long."

With a lascivious pause, Noah scanned her head to toe. "Maybe that wouldn't be such a bad thing, though," he said, his inflection enticing.

In the secluded isolation of a rain forest village, the whimsy of seduction seemed permissible. Being out of practice with such debauchery, however, Noah couldn't help but turn crimson.

Biting her lower lip, then licking her upper, Sabella pressed her cheek to his chest. She followed that with a deep breath and pouting lips. "I suppose, too, we should buy a few things for overnight. That is, if we are staying . . ."

Holding her tight and smiling to himself, Noah suddenly wondered whether Sabella had known all along that this would be an overnight excursion rather than an abbreviated escape. Then again, perhaps the change of plans was the inevitable surrender to the unrestrained forces now shared between them.

"Yes, we're staying. Aren't we?" Noah said without much reservation.

Another page had turned.

Increasingly unshackled, Noah spontaneously offered, "Let's head in—my tab. Shirts, pants, boots." Wearing a lusty expression smudged with a hint of perplexity, he leaned back and looked down at her feet. "Although I *do* like those high heels."

"*Your* tab?" Sabella retorted, staying right on script. "Chauvinist! Think you're in charge here? I may let you put it on your tab, but only if you admit this is *my* turf."

Noah looked around. She was right. His smile broadened, as did hers.

They headed inside the store and made their purchases. In addition to clothing, Sabella selected the appropriate articles for a forest excursion.

With bags full of items, they headed to Pousada Orquídea—the Orchid Inn. All the while, they played up the nuance of this being a clandestine escapade. For both of them, being in character meant simply being themselves.

The inn's foyer—embellished with bromeliads and, aptly, orchids—was old world, exuding fragrances that permeated the entire building. The concierge and desk clerk, one and the same, welcomed them with enthusiasm. After escorting them to their room and obliging them with a bottle of Muscat, he tipped his imaginary porter's hat, thanked Noah for his gratuity, and left the room.

Staring at each other in a room arranged with one chair, one chest, and a bed adorned with a white coverlet sprinkled with red hibiscus petals, they were alone. Looking about, they realized there was nothing implied nor left for the imagination.

"Nice," was all Noah could manage.

Sabella, not knowing how to proceed, held the wine bottle up to the window and read its label. "Excellent. This is originally from Greece."

"Oh, I didn't know you were a wine person."

She shook her head. "An oenophile, I'm not. It's just"— she took a protracted pause—"the Greek thing. Remember?" She turned to him, unsure whether to smile.

He walked over to her with a determined stride, his own smile certain and reassuring. "That's right. And that's okay. We don't have to hold back. It's us now. The past belongs to us. Most of it was good. Let's hang on to it."

He reached out and put his hands around her waist.

"Let's do it."

Her eyes widened; his face bloomed blood red.

"Open the wine, I mean!" he quickly added.

Sabella's jubilant laugh was just enough to entice Noah's face to resume its normal shade of embarrassment.

Sabella located two flowered plastic cups and a corkscrew on the chest. The items served their purpose well. Once their glasses were filled, Sabella pulled up the chair, while Noah sat on the bed. They were knee to knee.

He raised his cup. "It's not very fancy, but it's real. To us," he toasted.

The wine, a bit tart for such a sweet variety, was consumed as if it were a vintage French delight.

Sabella scrutinized her cup as if to check for legs. "Isn't it unusual how a wine, even this one, can have a pleasing bouquet and soothe the tongue when shared with—"

To finish her sentence, she stood, sat next to Noah, leaned against this new man in her life, and kissed his cheek.

In return, Noah placed his hand high on her side, drew her close, and kissed her on the lips.

With mutual reluctance—wishing yet not wishing to be perceived as overzealous—they parted from the embrace.

"I suppose we should get changed and get ourselves out to the forest," Sabella said matter-of-factly.

With boundaries of intimacy not yet charted, they chose to don their new attire while standing nervously back-to-back. Following a conciliatory pause, they obligingly turned face-to-face.

"Well, that was a heel-to-heel experience." Sabella's response was delivered with a captivating smile.

Both understood the ice had been broken.

Her sleeves were long, her hiking pants were firmly applied, and her over-the-ankle brogan boots created an image that set Noah back on his own heels. Noah knew he was not nearly as enticing in his hiking attire, though Sabella gave him a thumbs-up and an approving peck on the cheek.

Together, they made their way to the edge of town. The trees were towering and the fragrances refreshing. Noah, arching his back and craning his neck, looked up into the canopy.

Perfect, he thought. *This is the way it should be.*

They pressed on, entering the forest. Once again, Noah's memories brought him back to that day with Paulo and Durante. This hike would be a far cry from that first experience, yet he nevertheless remained leery. He was still out of his element.

Sabella took one look at Noah and his trepidation. Hands on her hips, she made a meager attempt to restrain her laughter.

"The rain forest isn't *too* dangerous—if you're careful about what you touch," she said with a joking growl while walking around a cashapona tree. Full of drama and jest, her eyes shared in the fun. "The chance of being eaten by a jaguar is *unlikely*. But poisonous spiders . . . well . . . touch 'em gently. Since we won't be walking through the water, at least you know the piranhas won't get you."

As an equally playful response, Noah gave her a penetrating stare, arms crossed, toes tapping. Passing behind him, she put her arms around his shoulders and kissed his neck.

They walked in comfortable silence for a while—Sabella at one with the forest and Noah now eagerly opening himself to it. Time was immaterial. Then Sabella stepped in front of Noah, drawing him down to her level by his lapels, face-to-face.

"The canopy keeps secrets," she said. "It hides this world we're walking through. This place belongs to only us. Our yesterdays made us who we were. Those days are behind us. They're gone. There's just us now."

With an overpowering, gathering look, she took Noah by the hands and kneeled to the forest floor. Before lying back on a cradle of leaves, she explored the protective canopy and only then extended her arms toward Noah as an invitation.

Conceding, he joined her.

She pressed her fingers to his lips. "This is our place."

Toward evening, Noah received his first lesson in fishing for piranha, using nothing but a wooden pole, a line, and a barbed hook passed through a wad of meat. Attracting the grisly fish was easy—Sabella showed him how to churn the end of his pole in the water. To most fish, the maneuver would be an alarm to flee; for the wily piranha, it promised a belly full of blood, guts, and anything else that might be wrapped around bone.

To accompany their entrée, they collected fruits and vegetables, the likes of which Noah had never seen. Reflective, he was pleasantly reminded of the comfort he experienced so long ago on his grandparents' farm. This was, once again, peace as it should be. He wished the day would never end.

Saying nothing, Sabella witnessed the serenity on Noah's face. She allowed him to remain in the present for a moment, then she waved a black acai berry under his nose.

"This will soothe your palate and quench your thirst. Does it still need quenching?" With a seductive smile, she brushed leaves from her pants. "Let's head back to the village. They'll prepare our meal for us. How does that sound?"

Not giving him a chance to answer, she placed the fish and fruit in his arms, then stopped to look back at the place where they had been lying. Nodding, they each smiled before exchanging a vivacious, satisfied look of approval.

Noah was about to say something when Sabella, reading his thoughts, simply said, "Yes, it was."

The restaurant, on stilts, overlooked a rivulet adjacent to the pier. Before entering, Sabella and Noah watched from the veranda as passengers boarding a ferry were surrounded by the same frolicking children who had greeted them upon their arrival.

One playful moppet offered a passenger a passion fruit flower. The passenger, wearing a backward-facing Yankees cap, swatted at the barefoot boy. Even from their perch, Sabella and Noah could hear the man growl an expletive.

Wincing, Noah jumped up and rushed to the rail, only to have Sabella catch him by the arm.

"Don't say anything. The kids are used to it. As for the creep . . . it's already too late. There's nothing you can do."

Neither of them needed to state the obvious: the man was an American. His air of superiority was as cocksure as the orientation of his hat.

"We have disgusting people too, just like him," she admitted.

"Yeah. As a kid, I lived by an Indian reservation. I saw a lot of this toward them." He nodded toward the American. "Unfortunately, I saw myself do some of it too."

Sabella gave his arm a little squeeze, then released it. Noah remained in his squared-off stance.

"Just the same, I'd like to kick his—well, you know."

"Yeah. I know. But forget him." She reached for Noah's arm again, pulling him back now. "It's our time. And it's time to eat."

As he turned from the rail, she thinly suppressed an approving smile and slowly licked her lips, clearly a double entendre that caught Noah's rakish attention.

As they entered the restaurant, olfactory delights welcomed them, as did an angel wearing a butterfly-print apron and a ring of flowers and eatables in her hair. Swaying to the music while looking directly at Sabella, the woman produced an explosive smile followed by a blistering hug.

"*É tão bom vê-la novamente!*" the woman exclaimed.

"*É bom ver você também!*" replied Sabella.

As an outsider, Noah couldn't understand their exact words, but he knew Old Home Week was playing out before his eyes.

Dislodging herself from the hug, Sabella stood back and pointed to Noah. "*Carmine, esté e o meu homem.*"

The woman's eyes lit up. "*Parabéns! Ele é um* bom *homem!*" She gave Sabella a congratulatory hug.

Sabella then turned to Noah. "Noah, this is Carmine," she explained. She nodded to the ensemble in the woman's hair. "Get it? Like Carmen Miranda?"

"I do get it!" He grinned and nodded continuously as he looked back and forth from Sabella to Carmine.

"Carmine doesn't speak English," Sabella added. "I told her you are my man. She said you're a *good* man. She thinks we're married. Is that okay?"

"Of course!" he said. Without hesitation, he gave Sabella an unexpected but assuring kiss.

Sabella, red faced and holding tightly to Noah's arm, punctuated the facade. "Well, now I'm sure she's convinced we're married!"

Carmine led them to a table overlooking a koi pond encircled by flowers, many of which were the same as those she wore on her head. Once the couple was seated, Carmine nodded at Sabella and patted Noah on the shoulder. A definite sign of approval.

Sabella held her arms in front of her, palms up. "My dear surrogate husband, we're in."

Noah took a deep breath, knowing he was a long way from Minnesota. At this distance, indiscretions were not only acceptable but legitimized and mandatory.

"I think you'll need a caipirinha," Sabella said. "My country's national cocktail. It has sugar and lime. Only offered in a jar." Her seductive quip was served up with a devilish smile. "Oh, listen," she said, turning her head toward the stereo speakers. "This music is popular during Carnival."

Noah, his knowledge on the fringe, offered, "I know this music. I like bossa nova."

Sabella laughed. "Nice to hear you know something of my country's music." She patted him good-naturedly on the hand. "It started in Rio, you know. A bunch of musicians, nothing highbrow. Listen," she said again. "'Desafinado.' It's by João Gilberto, a famous Brazilian singer and guitarist. And Stan Getz, the American," she added. "You probably know him."

She closed her eyes and began moving with the music. For that ethereal moment, the rest of the peripheral world dissolved away.

"João Gilberto is *O Mito*—the Legend." Her voice was soft and her eyes tranquil as she whispered, "He's my João's namesake. You may know Gilberto's 'The Girl from Ipanema.'" She blushed a little. "Sometimes I'd think of myself as the girl from Ipanema."

Noah reached out for her hand this time.

"Do you dance?" she asked, returning to the present.

Crimson again and momentarily frozen, Noah was the one to float back to the past. After a moment, he answered, "I tried to boogie once."

He was about to share his memory of a beautiful woman who owned a dance floor—but then he saw Carmine approaching with their meal.

"Remind me to tell you about it sometime," he finally said.

He added a wink.

It was well after dark when they returned to their room. They could still hear the music, soothing and muted, coming from the restaurant. With their French doors opening onto a balcony containing two chairs, they had a clear view of the water.

Noah sat with his arms over the balcony rail while Sabella stood at his side. Neither of them was entirely sure of a sequence to follow. Finally, Sabella began humming as she slowly stepped behind him. Swaying with the music, she massaged his back with her thighs. She squeezed and kneaded his shoulders before leaning down to whisper in his ear and run her tongue along his neck.

Consumed by tantalizing fragrances, mesmerizing music, and hungry caresses, they were in the same place, sharing and creating the moment together.

They remained at the inn for five days. Their nights were enriching, fulfilling, complete. They never spoke of love. Some things are simply understood.

Hand in hand, they stepped off the ferry in Manaus four days before the man known as Bento would return.

Chapter Twenty-Four

*For one impenetrable and rigid, a seminal event can
shatter the mold and transform the very soul.*

STEAM BOILED OFF THE TARMAC at Manaus International
Airport–Eduardo Gomes. The day was hot and muggy, just
as it had been when Noah first set foot in Manaus. Sweating
profusely, Jack mopped his brow as he and Noah sat in the
van outside of Terminal 1. This was the fourth day of their
stakeout. The inbound flight direct from Boston Logan
International Airport had just arrived. On its manifest was
the name Bento Cardoso.

Knickknack.

A flurry of passengers hailed cabs and buses for their
rides into the city. Among them, Knickknack was easily recognized by his swaggering gait and telltale fedora.
As if in some second-rate noir movie, he was carrying an
aluminum attaché case cuffed to his wrist. His German

companion was not with him, as the *Fuga* was not yet in port.

Wearing a lopsided chauffeur's cap and dragging two suitcases, a hobbling valet was close behind. Subservient in an attempt to placate his master, the valet bowed while fumbling to open the passenger door of the renovated gold Mercedes.

Anxious to leave and annoyed with his minion's bungling, Knickknack jutted his jaw. He raised his hands and, resembling a flamenco dancer, snapped his fingers in disgust.

Jack and Noah followed at a distance as the Mercedes left the lot, taking BR-174 into the city before proceeding directly to Sabella's home. With Sabella at the theater preparing for the evening concert, the house was empty.

Clutching the case, Knickknack wasted no time entering the house as his vassal remained outside, leaning against the car. Keeping out of sight, Jack and Noah watched as Knickknack soon reemerged from the house— minus one aluminum case. His driver jumped to attention. The Mercedes pulled away from the curb mere second later.

Jack and Noah did not follow. They knew Knickknack was being driven directly to the Teatro Amazonas, where he would receive his tickets and, as always, hand Sabella an envelope containing a sum of money just sufficient to satisfy her creditors, pay her tuition, and place food on her table. Keeping her only *close* to independence was imperative. Her land remained the gift that kept on giving.

Noah, who now had his own key, led Jack into the house. The door to Knickknack's room was locked, but Jack jiggered it in seconds.

He gave Noah an affirmative nod. "I've had other jobs besides selling bric-a-brac. Now you know the real reason I'm called Jack of All Trades." With a subtle wink embellishing a smattering of pride, he gently blew against his fingernails. He had made his point.

On the top shelf of Knickknack's closet was not one but three identical aluminum cases. Noah pulled them down and stacked them on the bed. Each case weighed approximately twenty-five pounds.

Protruding his chin, Jack passed his fingers over the latches. "Locked. These'll take a little longer."

His back against the wall, Noah craned his neck and peered out the window, making sure Knickknack didn't make an unexpected return. Jack picked the first lock in less than five minutes. Popping open the cover, Jack dropped his jaw and opened his arms in disbelief.

"Holy Jeezuz. Look at this. Bundles of hundred-dollar bills."

Leaving his post at the window, Noah thumbed through one bundle of bills. As he had long suspected, alluvial diamonds weren't filling the aluminum cases. Once all three cases were opened, Noah quickly estimated that each contained over a million dollars. Not that they needed it, but this was the final piece of evidence.

Wordless and expressionless, Noah stared at the bundles of money—blood money. Jessie. Abilio. João.

"Now what?" Jack asked quietly.

Without breaking his stare, Noah shrugged. "We go tell Sabella."

"Yeah, but *then* what?" Jack pressed, his brow raised.

Noah was silent for a long moment. "I don't know," he finally said.

Two pairs of trembling hands returned the cases just as they had found them. Noah and Jack relocked the door as they exited.

The evening's performance was well underway, with Knickknack securely nestled in its audience. The opera unfolding, *Elektra* by Richard Strauss, was a Greek tragedy, one of Sabella and João's favorites. It encompassed murder, madness, and emotional disaster. On this pivotal night, one member of the audience, although not King Agamemnon, smiled as he saw the carnage unfold before his own contemptuous eyes.

Jack and Noah knew they had time to rendezvous with Sabella in the lobby.

They found her at the ticket window, head bent down, methodically placing the evening's receipts in their respective drawers. Noah had to tap repeatedly on the glass before drawing her attention.

Looking up, she smiled as she saw Noah's nose pressed to the window. Leaning forward and peering through the opening, she puckered her lips and blew him a kiss.

Noah, eager, whispered loudly, "You won't believe it— you won't believe what Jack and I found in your boarder's bedroom. Greenbacks. Millions of 'em."

Initially bewildered, Sabella dropped her jaw and stepped back from the window. Striking a moment in time, she reconfigured. Now she was both angered and perplexed, with her teeth clenched and her head turning slowly side to side.

"Now what?" she asked.

Noah had to keep himself from bristling at the sound of this same question. As both Jack and Sabella waited expectantly, he ran his hands over his face.

"He'll stop by after the performance, right? To give you the envelope?"

She nodded.

"Don't change anything. Meet him as usual."

Grinding a clenched fist into his hand, Noah could feel something building deep inside. The same forces he had felt at the theater, when he first laid eyes on his Knickknack. It was then, on that very night, that he had crossed the Rubicon. Only now was he beginning to understand what fate, what decision, what act waited for him on this other side.

"Yes, meet him as usual," he repeated with no emotion. "And we'll meet him too."

Chapter Twenty-Five

Pretense: More effective when delivered wearing a smirk or a smile?

AFTER THE FINALE, EXUBERANT PATRONS filed through the atrium as they left the theater. Panning over the exiting throng, the man no one knew as Caubi immediately saw Sabella standing with two men he recognized immediately. He quickly winced. The fact that he recognized these men did not mitigate his surprise.

The older man was Jack Morris. Caubi knew very little of him, although he had seen him at the opera house with an aboriginal woman on more than a single occasion. Priding himself on being astute and presumably ahead of the game, Caubi saw Jack and the woman as insignificant fodder managing a shop cluttered with curios hardly fit for a shadowbox.

Fucking knickknacks. Caubi shook his head with disdain.

And of course, Caubi knew that Jack had been signaling to someone that one night at the theater. Most likely this young man, whom Caubi also saw sitting with Jack and the little woman out on the plaza on a different occasion.

The younger man was likely Noah Garrett, if Caubi were to believe the registration book at the Hotel Santos. The old clerk there had put on an admirable performance, and Caubi might have fallen for it had the book not been open in plain view.

Why these two men were interested in Sabella—that was as transparent as the ticket window behind which she worked. Why they might be interested in him, Caubi did not know. Yet.

But from a very young age, Caubi had always understood that being in control requires being close to one's adversaries. So he sauntered toward the trio. He saw everything before him as opportunity. There was no better time than now.

Calculated and poised, he caressed Sabella's hand as she obligingly reached for the envelope he offered. She then placed the envelope into her purse.

"A little remittance I have for you, Senhorita Sabella."

His smile turned her stomach, but she did her best by leaning forward to whisper a gracious "Thank you."

With a placid smirk and curling toes, Noah cringed inwardly. His heartbeat, initially slow, steadily increased. He was standing only inches away from the man he very well might have killed with his bare hands that first night at the theater had it not been for a fateful collision in this same lobby.

"Please introduce me to your friends," Caubi said to Sabella. It was delivered with a smile he believed was the perfect facade.

Hands were shaken and cordialities exchanged with Pickwickian charm. Caubi, none the wiser, perceived himself as being in command, especially when the young man was indeed introduced as Noah Garrett. From Caubi's perspective, everyone was most vulnerable when they were grieving.

Caubi extended his hands out to all three. "Perhaps you would be my guests for a cocktail across the plaza?"

Jack was first to accept the offer. "Well," he said, acquiring the role of the folksy American, "I, for one, sure know it's been a long day with a dry mouth. What the hell—let's go!"

Thankful to play supporting roles, Noah and Sabella merely nodded. They were silent as Caubi and Jack shared mutually fabricated pleasantries all the way to the nearby café.

Crossing the street, Noah relived the rainy night the little boy had been killed. A dichotomy: the innocence of a young child in contrast to the evil of the man now sharing his company. Reverberating in his mind was the thought, *There will be justice.*

Out of sight, looking out of the corner of her eye, Sabella gently brushed Noah's hand with hers. She let it linger just long enough to express the need for both of them to remain courageous and calm.

The foursome was led to a table by the window. Wishing to maintain a strategic edge, Caubi seated himself at the head of the table. He immediately then turned to Sabella. Without segue, he moved from lighthearted to dire.

The time was indeed now. Time to make his move. Caubi was at last in position. There would be no more "diamonds" leading to envelopes that had been keeping Sabella's bankers at bay. She would find herself in arrears. The bank would confiscate her property holdings. And he would purchase the land for himself—increasing the sale and distribution of his product tenfold.

It was time to rid himself of unsuspecting chattel.

"My dear Senhorita Sabella," he began, with a somber face, "I am afraid I have some unfortunate news for you— that is, if you wish for me to share it here . . . among friends." His face expertly lightened as he glanced about the table.

Sabella nodded. "Yes. Please. Any information you may have for me, I am comfortable with you sharing it here. As you said"—she tried to smile—"amongst friends."

"Very well," Caubi said. He then bowed his head respectfully. "As a preface, I once again offer my condolences for the incapacitating loss of both your friend João and your father."

The subtle inflection and the choice of terms did not escape Noah. One simply does not describe the deaths of loved ones as *incapacitating*. Noah recognized that resurrecting the issue of their deaths gave this snake the elevated position of consoler while keeping Sabella in the dependent posture of the bereaved. The resurrection also asserted his intimacy with Sabella as a display of male dominance—especially to Noah.

Noah's willpower to remain still was waning, but he knew he had to steel himself while listening to the "unfortunate news."

"Senhorita Sabella, you know that the land so beloved to the Almeida family has been under the scrutiny of bankers for many years. Gentlemen, you may know this as well. To our good fortune, I have retrieved alluvial diamonds from a tributary near this land. Bolstered by funds brought in by the sale of these diamonds, payments to the bank have been sufficient, though, well, marginal."

He made sure to wince.

"You must understand, Senhorita Sabella, that my men and I have done our best. But it now appears that we have sifted most, if not all, of the diamonds available in the region. I fear that unless we can find another source of funds, we will need to sell land to pay the taxes on the remainder of our holdings."

The three others sitting at the table clearly understood the meaning behind the words *we* and *our*. Nevertheless, they each managed to compose themselves with expressions of shock and worry.

Gilding the charade yet also wearing a mask of desperation, Jack leaned forward and grasped the man Noah christened as Knickknack by the hand. Looking up into the face that had betrayed everything holy, Jack made his plea. "There must . . . there *must* be some way to find more diamonds. There must be more! What can we do? What can we do to help?"

Caubi feigned hesitancy by furrowing his brow and shaking his head. "I don't know. I'm not sure there is any way to help . . ."

Noah turned his head, gripped with consternation as well as calculation. As he gazed out, it was only then that he suddenly recognized where they were sitting. This was the same curbside window table he and Jack had been sitting at on that decisive night. That night Noah realized who he was, where he was, and what he had to do.

This was where he had realized that he must, once and for *all*, put an end to what had become his proverbial Knickknack.

Noah forcibly pressed the heels of his hands to his eyes. To the others, he seemed to be in great thought. In reality—if reality could be applied to such a moment—he was not only planning but desperately trying to rid his eyes of cold rage.

When he pulled his hands away, he first hesitated, then looked at his palms before staring directly into the plastic man's eyes. "Please let me help. I have hands. I can work. I'll do anything. Anything I can."

Caubi stared back at this Noah Garrett. There was something about him. Not wishing to appear as if he were pressing, Caubi rolled his tone into the convivial.

"By the way, Senhor Garrett, you never mentioned your reason for being in Manaus. What brings you here to our obscure treasure nestled within the rain forest?"

Noah hadn't anticipated the question. He could only fumble. "Ah . . . I did medical training in Boston. It has several medical centers."

With the mention of Boston, Caubi's comportment immediately changed.

Leaning back in his chair, he looked squarely at Noah while slowly rolling a toothpick in his mouth. After a brief second, he crossed his feet at the ankles and resumed a pose of nonchalance.

"I see. But why would that bring you to Manaus?"

Stepping in, Jack gave Noah a fatherly—and at that precise moment, needed—tug on the shoulder. "I invited 'im. He's like a son to me. His old man and I were miners—in the States, I mean. Actually, mining's what brought me to Brazil in the first place. But dealin' in curios keeps the grime from under my fingernails."

Confabulating on the fly, he let out a hearty chortle.

"Anyway, I thought this poor young fella could come down here to have a little 'working vacation.' You know, work an hour here and there at the medical center but then kick back and soak up the sun for the rest of the day. He needs a break. I mean, look at 'im. He's been working his ass off!" Jack immediately bowed to Sabella. "Sorry about the language."

Caubi raised his brow and retracted his lips—a snarl tempered with a smile. He matter-of-factly shrugged his shoulders. The story sounded reasonable, and the two men did seem to have a certain familial dynamic. But with Boston soil still on his shoes, Caubi wasn't one to take coincidence lightly.

Not wishing to reveal his apprehension, he changed the subject back to Noah's offer to help. He rubbed his chin as if weighing his options. In truth, he *was* weighing them. Spending more time with Dr. Noah Garrett might serve its purpose. Wrapping up loose ends had its advantages.

"On second thought, perhaps an extra pair of hands and another set of eyes can't hurt. I suppose I could bring you to the site." Looking directly at Noah, he asked, "Tomorrow? We can leave early in the morning—say, six thirty? Seven? The only boat available is quite small. It'll carry just the two of us." He addressed this more to Jack than to Noah. It would be wise to separate the two.

Noah nodded slowly, his agreement building. Yes. Only the two of them. For Noah, the leaf had turned in more ways than one.

He looked at Sabella. Just as he had done that other night, sitting at this same table, Noah suddenly found himself overcome by a sense of calm. He watched Sabella this time. He saw her in another time, another place—displaying her coquettish grin, dark hair, and a come-hither wink as she, too, played prankster with the man she loved.

The world was right. Again.

He smiled at her. "My only river experience was on a ferry." She returned the smile.

Shaking his head a bit to clear himself, Noah looked back at the man who had taken so much from them all. "So, exploration off the Rio Negro will be new for me," he said with a healthy hint of trepidation. "But I'll give it a shot." His dependent role as a novice was purposefully expressed.

Caubi, adept at corralling naivete, was satisfied. Rubbing his hands together, he quickly stood.

"I must bid you all a good evening. I am to meet with friends now." To Noah, he added, "I will see you at the landing at seven. You might wish to have a hearty breakfast." He winked.

Noah watched him leave. With every step the man took, Noah's determination intensified.

The moment the man she still believed was named Bento had taken his leave, Sabella bared her fingernails and wrapped her hands firmly around Noah's neck. The force surprised him.

"He wants you on the river—alone!" she said in a castigating, jaw-clenching whisper. "*What are you thinking?* Mother of God—we know what he's capable of doing!"

Noah wrenched Sabella's hands from his neck. "I have to. He's done it to both of us. That's it!" He was concise and emphatic.

Jack said nothing, as if a commitment had already been set in stone. He knew it had, in fact. That other night at this same café. The irony of sitting at this table had not been lost on Jack.

Turning away, Jack summoned a cab that would bring Sabella back to her home, then drop Noah off at the Santos. During the silent ride, Jack turned his head to observe Noah. The young man wore a smile not sinister but nonetheless full of as much anticipation as Jack had seen that other night at the café.

Before Noah stepped out of the cab, Jack took hold of his wrist. "You're beginning to look . . . different. Something's changed. Again."

Noah looked begrudgingly into Jack's eyes. "Yes, my dear friend, it has. Nothing is forever."

Chapter Twenty-Six

For some, that ethereal entity responsible for the preservation of one's soul, delicate and nebulous, will shatter with a single stroke. Be it life's crescendo?

AT DAWN, NOAH MANEUVERED, with cautious intent, through the riverside market on his way to the landing. The rancid odor of fish lingered gnarly and pungent already at six in the morning. Although the gutters had been cleaned the night before and the piscine entrails returned to the black waters of the Rio Negro, the stench remained. It would become despairingly enriched with the incessant heat of the day.

Noah didn't know what the day had in store, yet he knew an irreconcilable course had been set. *Ashes to ashes, dust to dust* came to mind. Prophetically applicable for a dirge.

Workers scurried about the market, arranging their wares for the day. Some used tongs to carry large blocks of ice over their shoulders in preparation for the morning catch. It reminded Noah of the Laborville icemen who carried their burden up to his parents' second-floor apartment.

In particular, Noah was drawn to watch a shriveled old man with pick in hand, chipping slivers of ice into a metal bin. Clearly in his element, the man wore early-morning stubble and sat comfortably on his wooden-pallet perch.

In the clutches of the venue, unable to contain himself, Noah was drawn toward the man.

"That." As if giving directions, Noah nodded his head toward the ice chips. "I did that as a boy," he uttered as if momentarily transposed to another place, another time.

The man leaned back, casually flipping the pick from one hand to the other. With an attempt to muster a provocative smile, he slowly leaned forward, handing Noah the pick.

"Show me," the man said, more as a ploy, as he rose slowly and stretched his legs.

Noah was surprised to see a rhythmic tremor in the man's hands once he held them at waist level. The tremor ceased as the man proceeded to pull a pouch from his pocket and roll a cigarette.

"Be careful—it's sharp," the man quipped. An automated grin crossed his masklike facies as he ignited a match with his thumb.

Stoked by a challenge and comforted by a reminiscence, Noah set his tote on the ground and began chipping. Now blowing smoke rings, the old man kept a close eye on the young man, who appeared unusually skilled with his hands.

"Kid, *está matando ou lascando?*" asked the old man—Are you killing it or chipping it?

Without looking up, without stopping, Noah chiseled his intentions more than he chiseled the block of ice.

"Not bad. You've got the touch," the old man said. Then he clapped Noah on the shoulder—a universal goodbye in any language. "Time for coffee," he explained.

With his cigarette precariously dangling from the corner of his mouth, the man let out a yawn-enhanced groan as he stretched his back. His age and condition were exposed as he turned and shuffled away.

Upon his return, a few minutes later, the man found the block of ice reduced to splinters that now filled the metal box. The young americano was gone.

The ice pick was as well.

The 601 landing was next to a now-dry concrete ramp leading to the river's edge. By evening, it would be slickened by the remnants of tambaqui, arapaima, and bull sharks.

As Noah proceeded to the designated dock, he could see the gold Mercedes parked on a side street. Its elfin driver leaned dullishly on the fender.

Preconditioned to always be early or ahead of the game, Noah hadn't expected Beelzebub incarnate to arrive before him. In this venue, being the first to arrive had its strategic advantages. Clearly, Knickknack realized this as well.

"You're early, Dr. Garrett," a voice called out.

Surprised, Noah turned to witness Knickknack coming his way, brandishing energized confidence in his swagger. It was a noticeable difference from the disingenuous geniality he had displayed the previous night. He was smug, with tight lips and a plastic smile.

"We must be on our way before the river becomes too busy." Knickknack pointed to a small skiff tied to a mooring post. "Our vessel is seaworthy, yes, but tippy when passing the fast-moving barges. Barges have no eyes. We must remain cautious. We do not want anything incapacitating to happen."

There it was again: *incapacitating*. The same word he had used when describing Abilio's and João's deaths. The echo was foreboding. Revealing.

Making his eyes wide, Noah nodded. He chose to play the trepidatious novice, the same role from the night before.

After stepping into the boat, Knickknack dropped a small duffel, which clanked as it struck the transom knee beneath the motor. Noah followed into the skiff, giving a show of unsteady balance. Once seated, he leaned against the breast hook, where he could look squarely at Knickknack seated at the stern.

"It will take time to reach the waters where I sifted my diamonds," Knickknack said as he maneuvered the port, zigzagging among larger boats jockeying for position.

Noah took note of Knickknack's pronoun selection: *I* and *my*. It exuded an arrogance no longer tempered by risk.

"Our destination is a long distance from the comforts of Manaus," Knickknack continued. "You may wish to rest or even sleep."

Noah willed himself to sit motionless and expressionless as he pondered the river. He knew that if anything "incapacitating" were to occur, it would not be until they had left the main body of water. Too many eyes. But the tributaries, with their islands and inlets, would provide ample cover in which to dispose of anything. Or anyone.

Sleep wasn't an option.

"I'm fine," he replied. "Besides, I don't want to miss a thing. There's so much to see on this river. Different from the big one."

The big one—vernacular Noah savored, having initially heard it from a man he not only respected but revered for his directness and comfort with simplicity.

"Here, this river's black," he added. "Kind of foreboding, even."

This word selection brought a tempered grin to Knickknack's already austere expression. Any attempt to conceal his intent had passed. His conspicuous nonchalance was palpable.

Minutes, as if dead in time, passed in silence. The only sound was the agonal hum of the motor that caused the boat to vibrate. The resultant shimmy caused the duffel to slide beneath Knickknack's seat. With his foot, Noah made sure to steady his tote.

Looking toward the east, Noah watched the sun rise. A contradiction, as they moved toward a day that would be blotted by terminal darkness.

Eventually, Knickknack angled the skiff toward the northerly shore of the Rio Negro. Covered by thick overgrowth, the mouth of the tributary could be identified only by the red flag marking its location. Both men leaned forward, ducking their heads as the skiff passed beneath the tangle of branches that masked the entry. With high waters, there was sufficient depth to navigate the submerged tufts of land and floating morass around and between the trees.

Instantly, darkness swallowed the skiff. An electric river of anticipation coursed through Noah's body, branching into his fingertips. It would not be long now.

"We are very much alone here." Sotto voce, Knickknack's statement was not unlike a requiem.

Noah wondered whether it was inadvertent telegraphy or deliberate menace. In either case, it spoke to the same intended action.

Knickknack turned as if to tend the motor. His back toward the bow, he leaned forward, reaching beneath the seat for his duffel.

Even if there had been an ocean of options before Noah, it wouldn't have mattered. The diver had left the board.

Knickknack's head and arms strained between his knees as he pawed for the bag that had shifted during their voyage.

Noah had ample time to reach into his tote.

Ample time for one short step to the stern. That single step compressed each man's lifetime; eternity was about to take its first breath.

The onetime Little Captain came of age as he raised his arm. With surgical accuracy and without hesitation, he drove the ice pick between the back of Knickknack's skull and the first cervical vertebra. A ruinous scream reverberated through the canopy, disappearing into a sky that had lost its heaven.

Noah felt the tip of the pick skid off the base of the skull, then pop as it penetrated the leathery dura mater before entering the spinal cord.

Knickknack's back abruptly stiffened as he arched into an upright sitting posture. His arms extended downward as they became rock rigid. The pistol he had retrieved seconds before fell to the floor. Alive but barely able to breathe, he retracted his lips. His forcibly snarling teeth cracked as he made a hissing sound, attempting a frantic breath for air.

Noah twisted the pick, lacerating the spinal cord as if pithing a frog. Knickknack's eyes seemed to explode from their sockets.

Noah stood upright, assuming an overpowering carriage of calm even while his chest heaved. He glared into Knickknack's contorted face, the embodiment of the grotesque and vile.

"Bastard. You miserable bastard." His voice was slow. Calculated. Cold and lancinating as tempered steel. "You killed Jessie in Boston. You killed Sabella's João. You killed her father."

Stiff, helpless, his eyes pleading, Knickknack stared into the face of vengeance, of reckoning. Dread blistered from his every pore. Unable to swallow, he attempted to speak through froth bubbling from the corners of his mouth.

His last revelation: "You knew . . . all . . ."

Standing victorious, poised as a gladiator with pick in hand, Noah radiated an uncanny resolve. "Yeah, I knew." He paused. "Now . . . time for fishing."

With scripted finesse, Noah slowly rolled Knickknack's inflexible body into the water. Scarcely breathing yet alive, the man bobbed faceup as an inanimate cork between the trees.

Noah's face twisted into a sinister yet sanguine smile as he placed an oar in the water and began sweeping it alongside Knickknack's torso. In seconds, the river came alive, churning and foaming with piranhas. An expanding corona turned the black water boiling red.

Still cognizant, the man no one knew as Caubi Tomayo was surrounded by that which was him. His insensate body was being consumed as he watched—a voyeur unto himself.

Gitche Gumee never gives up her dead. Neither does the Rio Negro. The ghoulish figure disappeared into the acrid abyss. All that remained in the skiff was a fedora, a Luger, and a man standing with arms limp at his sides, very alone. A man never before seen.

Knickknack's last victim, the former Little Captain, was now at the helm.

Transformed, mesmerized, and accomplished, this new Noah stared into the water, wringing his hands. Somewhere within the interstices of his subconscious, he was reminded of the disfigured capuchin at Monkey Island—banished to the corner of the cage, bent, broken.

When you're not perfect, someone always pays.

Noah wasn't sure how much time passed before he turned the skiff and began paddling around trees. As if tapping into the collective consciousness of the river and the people who had called its forest home for millennia, he made his way back to the main body of water. The current then swept him downstream, back to Manaus.

Before too many boats and eyes surrounded him, he dropped the duffel with the pistol into the river. The fedora, though, he placed in his tote. Why, he didn't know—perhaps as an indelible reminder.

Noah returned to the 601 landing, then retraced his steps back through the market. The old man was once again chipping ice and smoking a cigarette.

As he passed, Noah dropped the pick at the man's feet and kept walking.

"Wondered where it went," the old man called out, exhaling a cloud of smoke. "Needed it, did ya?"

There was no response.

Chapter Twenty-Seven

Forever. Nothing is forever.

Perhaps?

WALKING THE RUA LOBO D'ALMADA as if in a dissociative fugue, Noah saw no one as he made his way to the Santos. Fragments of another life convulsed through his mind. In the distance, the image of a little boy in a sailor suit faded from view. Steeped in the righteousness of free will, a place he thought sacrosanct by decree, the Little Captain now found himself defrocked and, by choice, synonymous with everything abhorrent.

As Noah passed through the foyer, José, the inordinately gleeful host, reached out and gently tapped him on the shoulder. "Senhor. Your friend—did you find him?"

Turning mechanically, Noah delivered a hollow, obligate smile while holding reality at bay. Distantly, he recalled his conversation with José earlier that morning. Noah had told the man he was heading out to meet a friend.

"Friend . . . ? Yes, I found him. But now he's gone. Someone else's taken his place."

Sifting through his tote while trudging the stairs, Noah found his door key rolled up in the telltale fedora. At the end of the corridor, he studied the person in the mirror. He slowly turned his head from side to side. The image—distorted, wavy, and perverse—met his approval. A perfect likeness of the man.

He tucked the fedora back into his tote. "Now it belongs to me," he told his reflection.

He entered his room with newfound authority, as though he had never been there before. There was no doubt, an alien course was set.

Lying in bed, ankles crossed, hands clasped behind his head, Dr. Noah Garrett stared at the ceiling, mouthing words, codifying purpose and direction. After hours of measured apprehension, and with a reconciliatory narration completed, he fell into a catatonic sleep.

He was awakened by loud pounding on his door.

As an apparition, he rolled an angular body from the bed, shuffling across the room toward the door.

"He's coming," he said, referencing himself in the third person.

Trying to shake off the fog of sleep, he leaned against the door and unchained the latch. He peeked through the sliver opening. "Of course. Sabella. Jack. Flora," he said, summoning names for each face he saw. "He . . . I mean, I . . . Come in."

Sabella was the first to squeeze through the opening. She abruptly stopped once she saw the figure before her. As if thrashed by a reprehensible collage, her jaw dropped as she brought both disbelieving hands to her mouth.

"My God. Look at you. What's happened? We tried to call."

Jack, wide-eyed with a baffled stare, walked across the room. Shaking his head, he first looked at Flora, then Sabella.

"I've seen it before," he said. "I know what's happened." He looked piercingly, accusingly, at Noah. "Don't I?"

Remaining detached so as not to be assuaged, Noah answered, "Yeah. You do."

Astonished, Sabella held her distance, looking him over from head to toe. Then, guardedly, she reached forward and grasped his hands, attempting to lead him toward the bed.

He quickly retracted his hands, as though abjectly soiled, forcibly releasing her grasp. He stared at his palms, slowly bringing them up to his face. Turning his hands over as if seeing them anew, he finally looked up.

"You do understand—they're different now. That . . . that miserable creature I pulled out of a shadowbox, that goddamn *knickknack* . . . he'll never hurt anyone again."

With his jaw clenched and snarling teeth exposed, he raised his arm and viciously thrust it downward, once again implanting the pick beneath the skull of that wretched calamity. Staring at the floor, he wrangled a smile and casually looked up at his three appalled companions.

"That's what I did. That deplorable . . . *fucking bastard* . . . is gone."

Eyes aghast, Sabella shook her head and dropped her jaw. "I've never heard you speak like that before. Your language, it's . . ." She couldn't find the words.

Noah turned robotically, first looking at Sabella, then Jack, and last at Flora. Raising one eyebrow, slowly puckering his lips, he said, "Some things just change."

At last, Flora stepped forward. She reached up and ran her hands across Noah's face. Then she stepped away as if reaffirming that which stood before her. With both hands, she acceptingly patted his chest, solidifying the transformation: that which he was now.

"I remember your tears when you spoke with me at the shop that day. You were an angry, broken man then. Now you're simply broken. But you'll heal. It'll take time. A lifetime. But you will heal." Reaching down, she pulled his palms to her cheeks, as if his hands could restrain her uncertainty. "Possibly."

Tilting her head back, she reached up and gently placed her hand over his heart. For that brief moment, she shared something—understanding, perhaps. She closed her eyes, nodded, and smiled.

"You have amends to make, my dear friend. You're still a good man. Just . . . a different man."

Imperceivably slow, as if evolving through a mutable fog, he made an ethereal yet near-palpable separation from her, from them all.

"No," he finally said. "No options. Not now. Not for me." He took a deep breath and closed his eyes. "Keep it. The money. Split it. All debts paid. That is, except one."

When he opened his eyes, tears streamed down his expressionless cheeks. He looked at—through—Sabella.

"You were the most beautiful of God's creatures."

He didn't address her as the person sitting on his bed but as a person someone else had known a long time ago—in another life.

"The land. Yours. Finish your education. So many things . . . good things . . . you'll do."

"*I'll* do?" she repeated. "But what about—?"

Her question, cut short, didn't need an answer. The look on his face said it all. She knew he was leaving. She could see it in his eyes and in the cold void encompassing his body—the body of another person, someone she didn't know. The Noah with whom she had walked in the forest—he died, along with his dreams, on the dark waters of the Rio Negro.

She had shared true love with two men. And now they were both gone.

"I understand," she said quietly. "The creed's been broken. The creed that made Noah Garrett. Now you're like my father. I can see it. Like him, you feel salvation is no longer a part of you. It's retribution, isn't it?" Looking at him with a vague expression of understanding, she stood and pressed her index finger to his chest. "But *I* know there will be salvation for Noah Garrett."

Leaning forward, she kissed him on the lips.

"Goodbye. What I feel for you will be shared."

She turned and walked away. Looking back but one time, briefly, she smiled. Then she was gone. Into a new life and out of his.

Never to be forgotten.

As if directing himself in a lucid dream, Noah collected his things. Jack and Flora waited like stone sentries. At one with his persistent fugue, Noah then drifted from the room, down the stairs, out to their van. He heard himself ask to be taken to the long, narrow shop filled with bric-a-brac, where he would purchase a painting of the opera house—a painting framed with *Hevea brasiliensis.*

Suddenly awakening, Noah found himself standing in line, waiting to board a plane. He turned around. Behind the fence, a very tall man stood next to a Lilliputian woman. Noah knew their height didn't keep them from seeing eye to eye. He also knew that of all the characters in his life's saga, that woman retained the unblemished depth and insight from whence she came.

The plane flew for hours over an endless sea of green. Noah could see hell for some, but not for all. He came as one person, evolved into another, and left as a third.

Similarities?

None.

Chapter Twenty-Eight

Indentured, alas. Gone with a whisper?

. . . I MUST CONFESS, *Dr. Noah Garrett, I have never seen your face except through the eyes of my mother. I have never touched you, but you have touched and guided me throughout my life. She was alive and vibrant as she spoke of you and what you two shared.*

You were both different people before you met. You taught each other how to see a better world through new eyes—eyes that had once been tainted by preconceptions inflicted upon you by the worlds in which you were born, worlds of bias and prejudice.

I will always cherish and preserve your terra firma along the Rio Negro. It is now a sanctuary for the flora and fauna of the rain forest. It bears the cross of my mother's grave, as is the custom of the people of this beautiful land.

I am blessed, and for that I give thanks.
Yours with enduring affection and deep admiration,

Thomas Apollo Almeida

Sabella's last words to him: *My love for you will be shared.*
Now they made sense.

And with that, an old man turned his back on the Big-Sea-Water, the other inland sea.

"Thomas Apollo," he whispered.

Acknowledgements

I WISH TO ACKNOWLEDGE THE SUPPORT of my entire family and especially my daughter. As a gifted author, television producer, director, and writer, she gave unceasing encouragement throughout the process of writing this book.

In addition, Scott Tridgell—a computer genius—was always available to help with the technical aspects of putting words to keyboard to screen.

About the editor, Angela Wiechmann: Not only did she truly understand every nuance of the story but she also knew and understood each character and their purpose. Her editorial practice is to fully "immerse" herself in the very substance of her edit.

As a gifted proofreader, Kris Kobe addressed issues that may go unnoticed by a reader but that nevertheless enhance the rhythm and flow of the narrative.

The novel's aesthetically captivating cover and interior design are the products of Athena Currier. Athena brought this narrative's geographic location—as well as its double metaphor—to life. With the meeting of the waters, we see two rivers touch but not intertwine. Only later do they coalesce, under the power of violent forces. It is not unlike the characters in this novel. Thanks to Athena, this metaphor has been brought to our attention in the symbols that ease the flow throughout the text. Subtle, perhaps, though nevertheless appropriate.

I also wish to thank Alicia Ester and Beaver's Pond Press for their support in not only bringing this project together but bringing this novel to fruition.